Peter Zachary Cohen

MORENA

Drawings by Haris Petie

Atheneum 1970 New York

1549905

for Babe,
and Hunter, and Red,
with the best
of memories

1

THE HORSE SLOWLY AMBLING AMID THE HIGH, rough reaches of the Finger Hills was alone, because she had slipped through the busyness and the galloping and the shouting that had driven away the other four horses and the whole steer herd, a month before.

She was no longer as fast as the roundup, but she had lived for twenty-four years. She had learned that the startlingly loud waves of a man's hat were only the waves of a hat. She had learned to know when she'd be chased if she cut back, and when the ridden horses were too busy. She had learned which trees, in which draws, in which angles of the sunlight, would conceal her. Once hidden, she had the advantage of not being in a hurry.

She had not only avoided the roundup, but had escaped the deer hunters who had glimpsed her, and also the single, familiar man on horseback who had hounded her close for two days. She had escaped the hunters quickly, not knowing they'd turned back the moment a hoofprint and her fresh droppings had told them that what they'd seen was not a deer.

But the rider had several times forced her out of brush clumps, and into dodging gallops around them, and down through gully washes that made her strain and bruise her legs, until finally she'd found a place where he came no more.

"Stay here and freeze and starve!" he'd roared, though even to himself the rider had seemed to make scarcely any sound at all amid all the vast earth and sky. Then he'd ridden off. Out of his sight, Morena had rolled to dry off her sweat, and had laid down to rest, very wearied.

But now another familiar urging was upon her. She knew—perhaps from the lighter pressure of the calm air, or from the taste and swing of the winds that started and fell—that the first hard storm of the changing season was coming.

She'd begun walking. It was a slow, ambling, softly jolting gait: shoulders stiffly slipping frontward and back, hips rocking up and down in an old practiced rhythm. She was aware that, somehow, her rhythm was slower that it had once been, but she'd forget that and start to hurry. Then the ache of tiredness would start to grab her, and she'd slow down.

She kept moving along out in the open, following

the beaten, easy grade of a cattle trail up a hill, then deserting the trail, knowing it led down into a draw whose brush was thick, and the cattle-tunnel through it too low. She followed the crest, then went down and crossed where the bottom brush was thinnest, humped and struggled up the other side, and ambled on.

She knew every turn and stretch of the paths to follow. She knew where openings in every pasture fence would be, and that the air on the lower plains would still be warm, and the haystacks there fresh-smelling. She knew she was starting back closer to men. But every touch of the air, every instinct inside her, warned it was death to remain. She must leave.

Then something went wrong. The gateway from the upper pasture was closed.

She moved this way and that in front of it. She pawed a little, nervously and restlessly. In twenty-four years she had had to make adjustments before, and she remembered that. Off she went, ambling up and down the hills, following the fence line. But the other two gates on the lower side of the pasture were closed, too. And at the place where the wide, hard trail went through the open fence, there was always a big pit crossed by round bars that her hooves could not stand on. Twice she'd gotten her legs trapped down between those bars and the terror of that feeling she remembered well.

Back she came toward the main wire gate she was

used to, trotting a little. She carried her head high above the top wire of the fence line, as if trying to hear or scent amid the air's warning some hint of explanation or escape, or as if by seeing over the problem, she might get by it.

The main gate was still closed.

She lowered her head to scratch against her forelegs. She looked up and sniffed again, and pawed, and moved about, but never far. She could no longer gather the kind of strength to try jumping that high. Nor was she panicked enough to crash through it blindly. She was restless, but otherwise she was comfortable enough for the moment.

She pawed out clumsily at the gate with her front hooves. Then she pecked at the grasses a little bit one way, a little bit another, but she stayed close to the gate and the blocked pathway that led through it. She could think of no other direction to go.

The afternoon dimmed and grew dark around her. Over beyond the high rise of the hills behind her, the approaching storm rolled and blossomed and swirled across the earth.

2

AT THE MALLET CREEK CAMP GROUND, RIGHT where the high ridge timber dwindled out down the Finger Hills, two large, awkward yellow beasts started growling at each other. Then their headlights came on, and one behind the other the school buses began to slowly bounce along the rock roadway toward lower ground. The patches of embers left behind were drenched and mounded with the pebbly dirt and gave no glow. The back of each bus was piled high with tents and sleeping bags rolled up grudgingly, and thus somewhat sloppily. The night was the last of October—Halloween—and a spook, indeed, had caused this unwanted retreat: a spook in the shape of a little black box that had spoken with the voice of a man, a man forty miles away in the radio station at Belle Ore. A man with a witch's voice

7

that had cackled and sparked as he'd warned of heavy snow and high winds to come during the night.

The happy part was that it might make the teachers all late getting back from their yearly Friday-Saturday convention, but the combined Scout troops from Belle Ore and Alder Springs had groaned at the threat to the second night of their camp-out. They hadn't panicked, though. They had looked at the sky, tested the air, and decided there was time at least for the cookout—then the sing-out—and it was ten o'clock before the buses awoke and growled and left.

The rocky roadway soon became a little smoother and more gravelly. Then an eerie green needle on the dashboard of the second bus swung to the left; the bus immediately flickered its headlights and stopped. The first bus stopped, too, and the drivers got out and began a hurried conversation on the possibilities of an oil leak or perhaps just a crossed wire.

Lying cramped on a seat in that second bus, Alex Jaynes was especially hexed. Maybe it was a germ he'd brought with him, maybe it was the mulligan of hamburger, bouillion, mushroom soup, powdered potatoes, and powdered milk that he and Dale Logelin had used for their hurriedly cooked supper. But it was the greasy salt from the huge community bag of potato chips that he still tasted, and the sweet, half-cooled pop pulled from the creek.

The sick feeling had begun almost immediately after supper, and had kept at him so badly that Alex had passed up the first bus—the Alder bus—and the plans he'd had to spend Sunday with Dale. Dale could eat anything. But Alex'd gotten on the second bus, wanting only to get back to Belle Ore and to his grandparents for help. He'd pillowed his heavy jacket against the sharp window ledge, and wrapped in the cover of his light jacket, he'd sunk down across the whole seat. It had embarrassed him to claim such a privilege, and to let the misery show in his face, but that way he didn't have to try talking. The other kids had let him alone. They'd gone on with their talking and joking as if he wasn't there. And in the thick, awful air from the bus's heater his head had ached and his stomach had kept trying to throw the whole mess out on the floor, where it would stink accusingly at him the whole trip.

He'd held on while the bus was moving, and cool, clear air leaked in around the windows; but in the stagnant stillness of the pause, it became harder and harder. Around him the sounds of the talk and horseplay beat louder. The heat grew thick. Then the kids began to razz the delay by singing "Rolling home, rolling home, as we go rolling, rolling home—" louder and louder until finally Alex could take it no longer. He eased away from his seat and slipped out the door as unobtrusively as possible.

Outside, shielded by the darkness and the whirring

9

of a steady wind and the rumbling of the motors, he took five, six steps, found a rock to support him, and let it come. The rush of acrid tasting stuff filled his mouth and nose; and when it was done, his whole system kept kicking and sucking and tightening, and finally he threw up some more and then relaxed. Alex leaned back against the rock, feeling weak as a twig, and letting the cool, damp wind wash over him.

Then he saw Milt Toppen heading back into the Belle Ore bus, and Alex got up to go, too. When he moved, his stomach caught him, as if he were strapped to the rock; it squeezed in with a sharp breathless grip, and began retching drily; Alex gasped and hung to the rock, bent double; still nothing came, but his muscles tensed and his head thickened painfully with the pressure. Thinly behind him he heard the swish and grumble of the brakes being released and the bus starting up. It was a moment before the fright of it reached him, a moment more before the retching quit. He turned, saw the bus moving, and ran after it.

"Hey!" he called out, with a shout.

A roar of changing gears and a thick breath of exhaust drowned him under.

He leaped ahead faster, caught up with the bus's rear end. He hit his hand twice against it. Inside he could hear another muffled chorus of "Rolling home, rolling home, as we go rolling, rolling home—". There was lots of loose gravel being tossed up any-

way; his hand had made a noise, but not much of one on the heavy, rigid steel.

"Hey!" Alex screamed wildly this time, as the motor was gunned, and shot its exhaust at him, sourly. Very rapidly it was picking up speed, pulling just ten feet ahead, then twenty, closer to fifty, moving steadily, swiftly away, without stopping at all, but going farther and faster into the white sweep of headlights, the red taillights staring idiotically back at him. Alex finally stopped running; he simply couldn't believe it.

That was the first feeling, the disbelief. Then a tinge of panic, but Alex beat that quickly down with good humor.

"Well, nuts," he said, to an imaginary other self suddenly standing there inside him. "We're going to have to walk. I ought to yank out my stomach and make it walk, too. Why should I carry my stomach after it's done this?" He kept waiting every moment, for the bus to stop and wait for him.

It kept going.

The swift wind whistled close around him, not caring. The lights of the buses kept dashing and winking farther and farther away, silent and not caring. The ground felt hard beneath him. The stars were weak and few above the cool moistness of the wind. The friendly other self he tried to feel standing there inside him began to laugh: *'I'm* not really here, not really. You're all alone.'

3

HIS LEGS STARTED TO SHAKE. HE WANTED TO RUN. He started to run again. It felt good. He had on a single pair of socks in hiking boots that went only a little above his ankles, so his feet struck the road lightly. Very lightly, too lightly. The glows from the buses, flickering out of view for moments at a time, showed how fast they were going. He'd gone a few hundred paces. For him there were still thirty miles or so, down to the highway.

Well, that wasn't so bad. At least it was something definite to shoot for. And there were ranches closer, somewhere off along the road. But it was too far to run. It wasn't too hard to run in the dark; the raw gravel was a steady, duller gray amid the grass and sage. But it was too far. He slowed to a walk. He made sure he was calm. He was no greenhorn; he'd camped and hiked often before, and he started to think out what he should do. He looked up at the stars to check his directions, because the road twisted off on a big southward curve before going straight east to the highway, and it might pay him to cut across. The stars were gone.

He brushed at his neck, where something moist had kissed it. Then his cheek. Then his eyes blinked at something, and again. It was snow. The snow was starting.

Alex knew what would happen next: it would soon be so snowy it would make him dizzy. The roadway was going to disappear, first from sight, then from feel as the snow began to cling even among the tiny gravels. Not right away, though. How long?

Shelter, he thought.

With a tortured hope he dug in his pockets: some paper, a handkerchief. His sheath knife—yes! on his belt. But never mind that. He needed matches. Only he was remembering the horseplay before the sickness got to him, the matchsticks stuck in the big clump of moistened earth and set afire to make a burning skull shape. Not just a small skull but a large skull. "This'll frighten off the storm," they'd laughed. "We're getting our Medicine Man merit badge," they'd chuckled. It was all just a mad fling at the bad luck of having to leave.

It'd been fun, but if he'd known— If he could just run back and get his matches, before they all burned

— And his heavy jacket in the bus. But this wasn't a game. He couldn't call 'Time'. Already, as he expected, the snow was fluttering around him more thickly. The bus lights were no more. The air was turning vaguely milky, and all direction was gone. There was just the feel of the road, and that would go, too. He ought to wait till it paused and cleared. He had to hurry. The panic gnawed and pushed from inside him; he ran again, but the extra speed made him blinded worse by the snow, and he grew tired quickly, trying to feel and run.

Shelter! Matches! There were still some in his knapsack. Suddenly he started to think about the rest of his situation. His parents were at the teachers' convention and planned to meet him at Dale's tomorrow; so his grandparents weren't expecting him, but he'd told Dale that's where he was going. His camping gear was in the Belle Ore bus. They'd find it in town. They'd miss him that way. But it would take almost two hours to town in a storm; four hours before anyone could get back to him. He had only his light jacket to shield him, but he ought to stay out in the open on the road. They could miss him any moment. The bus might come back any time.

But he'd start freezing if he sat still very long, and he couldn't bear the thought of just jumping up and down, all alone, letting the time go by him, the snow pile deeper, and the wind chill into him. What if they *didn't* come right back?

He kept moving. He kept feeling along the road. The bus would come back any moment—no more than four hours—anyway, just thirty miles to the highway—less to some ranch. The snowflakes, swirling through the darkness, made him dizzy if he didn't keep closing his eyes or looking to one side. Their kisses had changed to tiny cold bites that stirred in him a useless anger.

Alex kept stomping ahead. His thoughts reached out to confronting Milt Toppen and all his Scout friends for just rushing and singing and leaving him; he saw himself walking in through town to his front door and showing his parents he was okay. His thoughts escaped into a dozen and two dozen picturings, and wore out, because the night and the storm kept tearing through them until finally he could think only about the wind and the cold gray darkness deep around him. He could feel every touch of his underwear, and down his arms and legs the chill scrape of his cotton shirt and trousers.

His emptied stomach knotted tighter around a mixture of fear and hunger; he began to notice again the bitter taste of his vomit. His head ached more and more with dizziness and impatience and tiredness and helplessness, and suddenly a leg jerked loose beneath him; he pitched sideways and fell into a free glide; he bumped on his seat, skidding on, head downward. He struck in a scraping mass of brush, and his weight tumbled him on over it. He rolled and slowed, hard, against some rock.

Alex got up on his feet, chill snow gobbed beneath his collar, and he felt something solid standing beside him. His hands were icy from sprawling in the snow but he could tell the bark of a tree.

It meant he was down in a draw somewhere.

He knew the road twisted to keep on the smooth high slopes of the divides. He had to have left the road to come near a draw—how could he tell just when or where?

It meant that he was lost.

4

THE LADY'S NAME WAS DEBORAH HANNUM, AND when she went into her kitchen to make sure the oven was off, before going to bed, she peered anxiously out the back door. Then she called to her husband: "It's started to snow, Marv. The radio was right."

Marv Hannum, comfortable in a big chair, deep in a magazine, mumbled, "Well, they can't be wrong all the time."

"I know," she answered. "But the old mare wasn't at the gate to the steer lot this evening, was she?"

"I didn't see her."

Deborah Hannum came back into the living room. "That's not like her. She's never missed coming in ahead of a storm before."

Marv Hannum muttered, "Maybe this is just some

flurries. It may not even be snowing up on the high pasture. That's ten miles from here."

"But the radio's expecting a big storm. You'd think they'd be bound to be right about a big one. And I imagine the nights are all awfully cold up there by now."

"Look—Debbie," he grumbled, "don't worry about that old mare. Nothing's going to happen to her. It'd have to catch her first. So it won't happen. Death itself couldn't do it."

"But she's getting old now, Marv. Maybe you ought to *bring* her in, or at least keep closer watch."

He sighed from deep in his throat and laid down his magazine. "I *did* try to bring her in. Two weeks ago I spent *two days* trying to fly over gullies and see around corners to catch her."

"You *did?* You never told me."

"I didn't have much to show for it."

Deborah Hannum thought about it for a second. She was a tall, thin woman, with a smoothly shaped face and dark hair just starting to gray. The hair was combed straight to fall and furl about the back of her neck. She said, "But if you were worried about her then, why aren't you worried now?"

"Why are you making such a fuss?"

"I'm not making a fuss. But Morena was the best cowhorse you had for fifteen years. So she ought to be worth fussing over."

"That talk doesn't make sense," he said.

"Neither does looking for her then but not now. Why *then?*"

"Look, Debbie, like you said she's old. She might not make the winter, anyway. Her teeth just keep getting duller. Her stomach and eyes are probably wearing out. She'll just start getting miserable. So there's no use babying her."

"Then why did you talk of selling her? Who would buy a twenty-four-year-old horse?"

He didn't answer.

"Brubain and Company," she gasped. "You'd sell Morena for nine cents a pound!"

"That would be ninety dollars, Debbie. That's a good start on a new colt just like her. It would be better than feeding her to the coyotes."

"No, it's not. You know it's not. Or you'd have told me what you were up to."

He didn't answer.

"Marv Hannum, tomorrow you better go up there. I don't care how deep the snow is. You better go find out why she hasn't come down."

"I *know* why she hasn't come down!" he burst out. He suddenly stood up. He was a strong man, without being terribly big; though no taller than his wife, he had thick legs and forearms and short, powerful hands. "Because I closed the gate, that's why."

"You didn't!" she exclaimed. *But of course he had, or he wouldn't have said it*. Plain anger sparked in her dark eyes now. "What for?" she demanded.

"Because I tried to help her, that's why. I got to thinking like you, that I ought to take care of her. I went to get her down here, before some storm caught her lame or something. As usual she the same as spat on me for a whole day. That was the night I talked about selling her. But I couldn't catch her the next day, either. So I figured if she wanted to stay up there and dig for grass all winter in twenty below, that was okay by me. Maybe after a little bit she'll calm down and come when I want her, for once."

"You got mad."

"How much bullying is a man supposed to take? I can remember plenty times chasing her round for a day, just to use her for three hours."

"I'll bet it would've taken three *days* to do the same work without her," Deborah Hannum said. " 'Calm but quick,' you always said. How many times have you come in talking about how she'd strike after a critter but never try to race it. How she'd never fought a bit in her life."

"Once you got it in her mouth. That was a half-hour corral rodeo every time," Marv Hannum insisted. "And a man risked his life every time he had to shoe her. Why don't you remember how quietly she'd let me trim her hooves flat so I couldn't use her barefoot, let me shape the shoe and all. Then she'd throw thunder-fits for the sake of ten minutes nailing. It used up most of a day every time."

Deborah stepped toward him easily, but she spoke

with a challenge. "It must've been worth it. You kept doing it. For years and years you kept doing it."

He stood steadily, his big, heavy hands on his hips. "Believe me, I know it. Three men couldn't keep a twitch on her, and if I'd tried to tie her she'd fought herself lame with rope burn. But I had to have her ready. She could be worked then. So I had to wrestle her way. How much dumb animal bullying is a man supposed to take?"

"And so now—" she accused him, "suddenly, with winter coming on, you get mad at her."

"No," Marv Hannum insisted. "I've been mad at that horse for twenty-four years."

5

ALEX JAYNES SLASHED AND STRUCK WITH HIS
sheath knife. The cedar stems sagged but clung to
the main branches with tough strands that he had
to yank and pull at to get lose. He attacked the sage-
brush on the slope, and it was tougher. He sawed
and sliced and hacked at it in the snow just above the
roots. His hands grew numb and aching with cold;
he shoved them in his pockets or under his armpits
while the damp shivers shook his shoulders and sank
in around his body. His stomach was trying to tumble
again, whether from bad food, or fear, or anger, he
couldn't tell. He held it back.

But the fear swelled stronger. He heard a torrent
of silent screaming; he felt squeezed and choked by
the thick, pale fussing of the snow in the night. The
wind scraped him. Something pushed hard on him to

run, to get away from there, escape from that cold that stung him everywhere. How good it would feel to run and yell toward his house and warm, quiet bed—go, run, run!

Alex's knees shivered to jerk forward, but he clamped them together. "No!" he cried out, and with his voice he tried to shatter the screaming he was hearing, and half-succeeded. He let his legs start stamping up and down in place.

"The snow—the snow—the snow—" he panted, barely aloud; his jaw was chattering and could not hang onto a whole sentence. "The s-snow will—will keep it warmer," he stuttered. "The snow—I'm going to make it. I'll—I'll live!"

He exposed his hands and went frantically at the brush, tearing and slashing, panting hard from the work, from the chill, from holding back the fear.

"If I just had matches— I've got wood— Paper scraps in my pockets—" He forced his voice out louder; the voice helped, it was a fist against the storm. "Boy—If I could just— Reach in for a match — But I've got the old knife— What if I didn't—!" The thought was stunning. He stood stock still at the horror of what it would be without the knife. "But I've *got* it—I don't have to worry about *that*—" He jumped back to work, with swift, over-anxious grabs. "Only don't lose it— Careful!— Don't lose it— In the snow—"

Gradually, he got brush loosened and piled. He

got cedar boughs tangled to it. When he crawled down amid this homemade briar, the wind overlooked him. But the snow clung to the outside. It built thicker and more solid and snug against it.

Alex tried to relax, but more stomach spasms sent him up and flopping forward. It was the dry heaves again; he went through it buckled down in the snow. When it was done, he crawled back, chattering, squirming against the chill.

The wind still whistled, and the snow still dimly flickered down in front of his shelter. But he found that the screaming fear had been walled out. If only there were a fire.

"Come on, snow; come on, snow—" he breathed aloud. "You see—" he spoke aloud, to that other self he wanted to come join him, "the clouds'll keep off the bitter cold—After daylight they'll find us. It'll take two or three, maybe four hours after daybreak —and they'll be up here finding us."

"I wonder what time it is." Again he spoke aloud. "Probably not as late as it seems. Probably longer to wait than I hope. I wish I could sleep."

Lying cramped in his hollow he stretched and worked one arm and leg at a time, and shivered anyway, and sneezed. He moved less; he was worn out and he dozed, and woke up aching and squirming against the damp chill. He wanted help. There was none. The gray darkness kept on. "Daylight—" he wished.

6

HE NEVER KNEW WHEN THE DAWN CAME. IT WAS well-started before he realized that the snow all around him was no longer pale gray against blackness. The snow was white. Dull white. He could see tree trunks out through the small flakes that were still falling. He could see through to the draw's bank across from his shelter, and the solid white snow there all rumpled by the brush underneath.

He saw it all without stirring. He was very stiff. His bones felt like icicles imbedded in him. Yet it was a peaceful chill, as calm and steady as the gentle flitting of the snow. He felt actually used to it and didn't want to stir. With his hands tucked in against his body, and his legs drawn up, he was as comfortable as he could be. And he was tired. He thought he would just lie there and wait for the sounds of a motor up on the road.

Yet the more he thought about how comfortable he was, the more he felt one little cramp, then another; the more he wanted to stretch. He moved just a little, and then he exploded outward from his shelter, floundering into the snow, stumbling with stiffness, finally standing up. He felt anchored by two numb and heavy rocks. He had felt them the moment he'd moved, and he'd known enough to be startled. He knew he had to get the circulation back in his feet. He'd read how the first sign of freezing to death was a pleasant drowsiness.

The fear started to churn back in his stomach and howl at him out of the wind rushing over the draw.

"Let's get busy and do something!" he urged himself. *Come on,* Alex tried to wake the other self inside him, but it didn't respond.

Alone, Alex forced himself into heavy tramping along the draw's bottom, lifting and dropping each numbed foot like slow hammerstrokes into the knee-deep snow. There was just enough tingling feeling still in them to keep him from panic. When he stumbled against hidden roots and stones, there was pain that burned sharply in his frosted toes, and there was nothing to do except wait till each pain burned out.

When he checked behind him, his shelter was gone. There was nothing at all like it in the flickering fog of snow.

He mumbled, "If I went back closer I'd see it. If I stay in this draw, I can't get lost."

He kept following the draw's bottom uphill. It felt uphill. With the snow all wrinkled and drifted, it was hard to be sure. He judged by the look of the trees, and by the shape of the snow-filled washouts.

"This must head below the road. If I know just where the road is, I'll know how to listen for them. I could leave a signal. It can't be far."

It wasn't. What a joy, amid it all, to be correct! The draw narrowed, and ended against a great white slope of brush and snow that widened upward into snow haze. It was like the places he'd seen in movies where dead heroes were shown disappearing into heaven.

"The road must be right on top," he said, aloud. His jaw had exercised itself freer, but his voice went out into the snow and wind-sigh like a hollow puff. Yet perhaps something had heard him. He couldn't imagine what. Ghosts, maybe. Wolves. The fear was still nibbling at his edges. He wanted to climb up to be sure of the road and leave some sign, but he didn't dare disappear into that whiteness. The draw was his friend. It had definite shape. Its trees were cold and dark and not smiling, but he could see them, and they'd give him anything he could take.

He began shuffling back down the draw. His feet were just beginning to limber. He paused to fill his mouth with snow, and then sucked on a twig.

"They'll be here before I really need food," he said. He kept talking out loud to himself, because if he had someone to talk to it felt as if he had someone to help him. Yet when he found the cold, dark shelter again, and tried to make it tighter and snugger, he worked in a loneliness where nothing moved for him unless he pushed, or pulled, or tore, or stomped it; and where everything waited, ready to collapse in a puff of snow. The snow still flickering down kept a vague, dizzying ache in his head, and its icy touch burned his raw hands for every thickness of shelter he added.

"It's not worth it," he grumbled, and tried to quit. "It's not too long to wait now." But the storm was still all about him. He couldn't stop and just let time go by him. He couldn't take any chances. Then he sensed a loudening growl in the wind. He raised his head in alarm. His head seemed clearer. The snow flickerings had stopped.

Above the draw he saw thick, heavy clouds sweeping past. He could tell earth from sky. He began charging up the draw's bank. The higher he scrambled the more sharp the wind sounded, the more swiftly it whipped at him; but the snow had been blown shallower. His feet could lift easier. The draw's bank bent into a gentle, endless rising ahead of him. At last he stood panting and shivering on the crest.

He saw the gullied hills in big spreads of white and folds of dark raising up into the clouds. But nowhere could he see any unnatural curves or lines that would mark the bed of the road.

"It's got to be there," he said. "Sure, it's got to be right up there somewhere. I ought to go find it and leave a sign. Except, how far is it? I'd be out in all this wind. Hey, clouds, you wouldn't suddenly start snowing all over again, would you?"

They might.

Undecided, Alex turned to let his eyes explore the other way, and squinted into the vast, glimmering grays and whites where the hills sank lower and lower beneath the giant, clouded sky of the plains.

The straight unnaturalness of a nearby fence line caught his sight, and then at the same instant that he located some dark, heavy brace posts, he noticed a horse.

That moment flared and passed, without words. It was indescribable. Luck. Warmth. A chance right there waiting for him, to find the road, to go, escape.

But Alex was no greenhorn. He knew some horses were friendly and some were not. It might bolt off if startled. Yet the horse ought to be hungry, too. The way it stood by the gate showed it.

Alex ducked back, and started following the draw toward the fence line, dropping steadily downward to the middle of the draw's slope where the grass would be the tallest. He kicked and dug and slashed in the snow there. He tortured his hands till he had his pockets stuffed with grass. Then he wouldn't let himself go on till he'd stuffed his shirt, too. It might all depend on an extra handful of grass . . .

7

Milt Toppen felt for a moment the chill dampness of the falling snow and then, Sunday paper in hand, he retreated into his living room.

He was a soft, somewhat paunchy man. He had soft tan hair that was neatly combed, though growing thin. With a great deal of comfort and satisfaction, he settled down on the thick sofa, and his wife, a soft, pleasant lady in a quilted pink robe, brought in a table-tray fragrant with oatmeal, freshly-cooked eggs, and buttered toast. She sat beside him.

"It's really snowing," she observed pleasantly.

"Eight inches, at least," Milt reported pleasantly. As he spoke he scooped a spoon deep into the oatmeal, and his eyes gently scanned the first columns of the newspaper. "It must have come down hard for a while sometime," he added.

"Didn't you have any of it on your way home?" she asked quietly.

"Nope, we beat it in clean," he answered proudly. He spooned the oatmeal into his mouth and flavored it with a bit of toast. His eyes flowed unhurriedly into the next columns.

"It's a good thing you came in when you did," she complimented him.

"I'll say," he agreed. "I suppose some'll claim Len and I didn't bring those kids in early enough." Deftly his glance sank line by line through a news story near the bottom of the front page. He was used to spreading his attention: during the week he mostly barbered, but he also owned the automatic laundry in Belle Ore, and the one in Alder, and he owned a bus that the Belle Ore school, and sometimes the Boy Scouts and others, hired him to drive. "Heck, we couldn't cut the kids' camping trip short without giving them part of an evening to howl in," he said, lightheartedly.

"Of course not," she said. "Did they really howl?"

"Oh, did they!" he answered. "They horseplayed and storied like Injuns." He moved the first section of the paper over so that his wife could scan it, and he began to look at the front page of the next section. "Scout Johnsbury burnt his thumb, and Scout Jaynes mixed so strong a mulligan he decided maybe he'd better come home instead of going to Alder with one of his friends. But otherwise, no casualties."

"It *is* a business with boys." His wife grinned, with fond amusement, and began to read the paper. Suddenly she looked up. "Alex Jaynes' folks aren't here, are they? They've gone to the teachers' meeting."

"He went to his grandfolks," Milt Toppen reminded her patiently. He forked some scrambled eggs onto toast and began savoring it all together.

"Of course," Laura Toppen said. Then she smiled again. "I wish I'd been an owl last night, way up high, so I could've seen all the porch lights snapping on, all the sleepy, worried parents opening front doors."

Milt Toppen laughed, too. "Tiredest bunch you ever saw. Whooping and singing when we left; hardly a whisper when we got in. Len and I could've gone to sleep standing up at the curb, just leaning against each other. What we let out of that bus was just a bunch of Scout uniforms stuffed with sleep. I noticed that one of the kids had left all his gear just stacked in the bus."

"I can imagine," his wife nodded. "Whose was it?"

"Well, I don't know. I was too tired myself to check then. And it'll be better for the kid to think of it and check on it himself."

"Yes, I suppose that's true," his wife agreed. "And in the meantime," she said, "we can wait and make private guesses as to whose boy we think it is."

"Okay," he said. "And sometime I've got to go out and guess what's started my oil pressure gauge to act up, off and on.'

Then soon, his breakfast done, Milt Toppen slid away from the table-tray and sofa and down onto the floor. It was easier there to spread out the inner pages of the paper.

Milt Toppen was a busy man—that was how he paid his bills—but he'd learned to let things take their turn. On a Sunday morning, he liked to lie down and spread out the paper and let the storms of the world pass over.

1549905

8

ALEX FELT THE WIND WHIP AT HIM AGAIN, THEN grab at him, then swallow him whole as he tromped up out of the draw. It was a stronger wind than the one that had brought the snow, and now he was facing into it. It scraped his eyes so that they watered and blurred, and hurt his ears so that he tied his handkerchief around his head, but the wind went through it; then he dug his cold hands back deep in his hay-filled pockets.

Yet there was a little more spring in his legs. He didn't feel bad. Even the gray morning was cheerful after the hard and hostile night. He began telling himself, with amazement and pride, that he'd survived a night snowstorm out in the wilds all alone, with only his hiking clothes and a sheath knife. He felt that soon something—most likely a game warden's truck—would be beckoning him into its warmth. Meanwhile, that horse was standing there out in the open, not half a mile away.

He stayed upright, betting he had a better chance that way than trying to cover the distance creeping or crawling and looking like some animal no horse had ever seen before. Patiently and steadily he plodded ahead, through snow nearly as deep as his boot tops. He experimented with bobbing his head up and down, thinking he might accidently resemble another horse that way. With the wind pouring at him, there was no chance of the horse catching his scent.

The horse stood facing him, its head dropped low in the windbreak protection of his shoulders. Alex hoped that it was not a stallion, and the thin look of the shoulders seemed to promise it was not. Gradually now as he moved, he reached under his light jacket and unbuckled his belt and freed his sheath knife. He put the knife into his hip pocket, handle down to help keep it from falling out. He left the belt loose in its loops, ready to be slipped out and around the horse's neck.

He was about halfway to the horse.

Suddenly it looked up, ears perked.

Alex stopped stiffly a moment. Then, thinking steadiness would work best, he moved on.

The horse stirred restlessly, but not much: a few heavy steps away, a few back closer.

Alex moved closer. He could see the coarse fuzz of the winter hair. It made the horse look orange-colored. He kept moving closer. The horse ambled slowly away from the gate, turned its rump toward him, then stood eyeing him back around one shoulder. In spite of the thick hair, as it had moved, Alex had seen the rippling of ribs. His hopes rose higher; everything—the ribbiness, the stirring about minus any crowhops or short quick dashes, the bony thrusts of the hips and withers—all spoke of age and a bigger chance of gentleness.

Then the horse broke away and in a slow, jolting trot curved wide around him, swinging back into the wind over a hundred yards away, and stopped, with her forelegs wide, and her head stretching cautiously down to sniff at the trail he'd made. The trot had pleased Alex for he'd seen by the smooth belly line that the horse was a mare. And now she seemed calmed by the man scent she was finding. She only stood with her head up and stared. A brown horse; solid brown, blurred by an orange fuzz.

Alex stared back, equally baffled wondering what to do next. Then she started ambling toward him.

She stopped about thirty yards away. She looked him over. She saw none of the lose, thin ends that meant ropes or bridles, nor did she see or smell any buckets of grain. Alex started to bring out a handful of cut grass, and at that first motion she lunged away into a lope, which slowed into a trot as Morena headed upwind for the concealment of a draw, a quarter mile beyond, where she had sheltered through the night.

Alex saw her direction, and then glanced up the open slope, and seeing no sign of any vehicles, he began to follow. He began planning that with bluff and shout he might corner her there.

Morena reached the draw well in the lead, but swerved away from re-entering the deeper snow. She put her trust in open distance, and again trotted in a wide curve around the man, and was disappointed to find that the gate had not been left open behind him. When the man started back toward her, the message was clear: she was being chased.

Alex had gotten a message, too. "She wants out of here as bad as I do," he said to his other self that suddenly seemed to be there with him. "We could get out of here together, easy, if she weren't so trotting dumb!" he complained.

"Easy now, you're just starting," said the other self.

The gray morning was becoming brighter, a gray brightness beneath the clouds, and even a bit warmer. Again Alex looked upslope to where the road ought to lie, lightly hidden by the snow, and he looked off southward across the slopes toward where, last night, the buses' lights had gone winking away.

He felt a tinge of worry that he saw no movements, except for puffs of snow flurried up by the wind. But he told himself a plow would move slowly; they'd probably have to come behind a plow. And maybe the low clouds were still snowing down on the plains, or the wind had left deeper drifts there. Actually, it was probably still early.

He dug out two pocketfuls of the fresh-cut grass and went toward the mare, offering the thick handful ahead of him.

Morena understood the offering and jogged away. Nearly always through her long life, food offered close by a man meant getting caught, and getting caught had meant more work than food.

But again she didn't run off far. She wasn't too nervous when she couldn't be caught, and she knew that men on foot couldn't catch her in the open. She trotted around the man again, then went loping past the gate again.

"Keep after her," urged Alex's inner self. "Don't let her get away with that. Wear her down."

Alex tried staying slowly and steadily behind her; he tried talking low and soothing to her, though his voice, out in the open, sounded awfully small and weak. The mare simply paced away from him.

She never went far. Morena was hungry. She was aware of the constantly changing weather. She already sensed the newly rising air pressure that spoke of a clear and bitterly cold night ahead. She knew that beyond the gate she could work her way lower and lower to more feed and warmth.

Now Alex was jogging after her, trying to cut across her circles, trying with waves of his arms to crowd her against the straight fence, trying just by doggedness to will her down. Sometimes he got close enough to hear her insides jiggling. He took off his handkerchief—maybe that was spooking her.

The haystacks she knew of, the frigid night she expected, these were just vaguenesses in her mind. The man was real and nearby. So Morena made no compromise. She would not give up her freedom to get through the gate.

Alex's own empty stomach began to gnaw and drag at him. The grass he'd cut became an aggravation. He couldn't throw it or shoot it. He just had to hold it out and beg. The continuing lack of success weighed him down. He quit.

Then that inner self mocked him: "Time goes slow when you just stand around waiting. You don't reckon you're not good enough to catch her, do you?"

"Look," he said. "If I'm going to do all this moving around I might as well find that road and start down it."

"You can't make thirty miles, not through fresh snow. It's probably fifteen to a ranch, if you can find one."

"I won't have to; they'll be coming to meet me."

"Okay, if you want to get rescued. Me, I'd rather be making my own way, and only get helped."

The idea stirred him. It was early, and warmth

was rising with the daylight. He was sure someone would be coming before long. In fact, there'd be lots of people searching for him. The whole countryside would be out to help Alex Jaynes home. And the questions would start: Why'd you let it happen? Why weren't you better dressed? Why didn't you have any matches? Sure, he'd gotten through the night by himself, but it'd be better not to be just waiting helplessly. Getting stranded without matches or food or enough clothing bothered him too, just thinking about it, without lots of people asking him questions to make him look like some kind of infant.

He wanted to joke about his mistakes. If he had that horse and was making his own way, then he could laugh with them. He'd be as good as anyone who met him.

He looked nervously across the long white slopes hoping not to see anything, not yet. He wanted to catch the horse and be safe and riding her before they reached him.

9

ALEX SET DOWN HIS THICK HANDFUL OF CUT GRASS. Then he took more from beneath his shirt and slowly backed away, leaving a trail of bunched handfuls for twenty or thirty steps, till he was emptied, and he stopped. He waited. If she'd just settle down enough to eat, he might be able to walk up to her.

Morena was used to having winter feed spread on the ground for her. Usually from a truck, but not always. Sometimes the feed would be spread toward a corral, and she'd learned there was often work connected with that. She could see there was no corral. She went slowly forward; stopped. She held her head canted off to one side so she could see forward and backward. Then she started a little closer, stopped again, but finally got in reach of the first bunch of grass. She stood with her hooves planted and her legs and body leaning stiffly back away from it, while her neck and head strained down toward it.

It looked like hay, but the grass reeked with man scent and she snorted and heaved away from it, snow puffing up from the heavy pump strokes of her feet. She took herself in a long circle again, swerving back so sharply she slipped.

She came so near to falling that Alex's heart skipped, and he started to charge to get his loosened belt around her neck. But she held her balance and went trotting directly to the gate again and paused there till Alex came too close.

Alex gave up coaxing. He went jumping and racing after her, whooping and yelping, no longer trying to calm or bluff her against the fence, but trying to keep her constantly moving and making turns so she might get careless and slip again. She kept wanting to come back to the gate as he'd hoped, and she was stumbling, all right; the snow was packing into clinging round-bottomed balls beneath each hoof, and then unexpectedly they'd break away. But she had too much speed too easily, and just began wearing a smooth circle around him in the snow. He tried to pack snowballs to interrupt her, but the snow was too crisp; it took him too long to beat a mass of it soft enough. Alex grew short on breath, but comfortable, even warm at his work. He noticed the wind had slowed down, almost to a stop. The horse kept going round and round with wet squeaks and rattles from her insides. His legs were leaden; his breath finally played out. That other self laughed at him and said he looked like a miserably misplaced circus act.

Then, suddenly, a spotlight shone on him. A second bright glow awoke nearby. Then a third—

Sunlight! The clouds were breaking up. Wherever the sun's gleam struck, the snow now glittered with pins and shards of bright colors. The dawn had been cheering after the dark but this was gay. It lifted the lid. More and more—wondrously and tremendously —the bright blue broke through above, and spread wide; the tops of the hills began standing out clearly against it, and catching the gleaming light. He could see to the edges, and it no longer seemed a challenge just to stay alive. Alex could feel the extra warmth shining down, even when the wind gusted up again.

Bright with new spirit Alex tried again. The horse just went round and round him. His legs stayed weak, and in the bright glaring his head soon began to ache and grow dizzy from his lack of food and good sleep. With a gasp of missed breath he stood still, suddenly realizing what the sunlight was telling him. He watched the small shadow the big body of the horse was making. He saw his own shadow hugging close around his feet. It wasn't early any more. It looked scarcely an hour till noon.

Morena stood still, too. Whatever was being done, she seemed to have it under control. She wasn't being caught. She began poking toward the first bunch of the cut grass, which seemed a safe distance away from the quiet man now. She put her head down, and hungrily munched at it, while keeping an eye on him.

Alex didn't pay her any attention. At this time of year it got light about six. They'd had at least five hours to come forty miles from town. If they'd missed him last night, they'd have been here at dawn. Someone would. Those big plows could get through this storm. It wouldn't take this long. Why weren't they here? Had he missed seeing them? Had this lousy, rotten horse kept him from seeing them?

"Where are they?" he cried out aloud. He shouted it at the bright, sharp-edged, empty spread of hills. He shouted sharp and clear to himself.

"It's warm now—!" he cried out, loudly. "But in three hours it'll cool off. If it stays clear, it'll get fifteen or twenty below tonight. I can't get through that like this. Even if I do, my feet and hands'll freeze. My ears, too. And I'll lose them. They'll have to take them off. I don't want that. I don't want it!"

He felt the urge to run. Again he held on. He didn't know *where*. The sky horizon he could see didn't look like anything he could remember. Yet the sun assured him of where east was: down the long spread of cut and wrinkled slopes. The highway was down there. Should he try to head straight for it, or follow the big southward loop he knew the gravel road made?

Maybe the buses'd gotten stalled or wrecked. He

had a dizzy dream of stumbling onto it and somehow saving everyone, just by his being there. The dream dried out in an instant. All that mattered was that no one was coming. The day was late. Somehow no one was coming. He was going to have to save himself.

He kept talking, low and steady and hurried, spelling things out. Six hours till nightfall—all the snow; he'd still be able to see by snowlight—thirty miles to the highway. He could guide to it by the stars. He might wander farther than that looking for a ranch house. At least twelve hours of walking in fresh snow, snow nearly up to his boot tops in the open, and up to his knees in the draws, if he short-cut straight east. Midnight. Probably it'd be closer to three or four in the morning. The cold would be down hard by eight o'clock tonight, long before he could make it. His feet and hands and ears would freeze long before he could hike it.

He looked again at the mare. To catch her now was a serious, deadly and desperate need.

10

He stopped talking aloud.

Quietly Alex began to count up what he had to work with: the belt loose at his waist— His hand shot to his hip: the knife was still in the pocket!

There were miles of fence wire. How could he use *that?* He couldn't get close enough to the horse to throw it like a lariat even if barbed wire might work that way.

A trip wire, he thought. To make her fall. Where? In a draw. She wasn't running into any draws. He doubted he could chase her in. Then at the gate. What if she jumped it? She'd get through—she'd get away. He wouldn't let her jump it; he'd snare her. He had to catch her at the gate. It was the only place she'd come close to.

Alex attacked the gate with his knife. The gate

was four lengths of wire stretched across four thin, loosely standing poles; each end pole was held to a fence brace by two loops of wire. He pried at the staples that held the next-to-top gatewire to the thin gate poles. The knife point broke off, a half inch back, and he cringed—but it didn't matter, he couldn't worry about it. He kept prying and got the wire loose. He untwisted it from the end gate poles. He pried one of the two middle gate poles free from all the wires.

The old mare finished picking up all the cut grass he'd left lying on the snow, and he stood watching.

Alex bent and tied the loosened wire into a circle that had a tail. He wrapped the tail about the gate pole he'd freed so that the circle looped out beyond one end.

Then he snapped off another little triangle-shaped piece of his knife blade, but he got the bottom gate wire unstapled, too; he tied it to the middle gate pole he'd left standing, and tautly from there to the nearest fence brace. Then he slipped the latching loops from the gate poles at that end and made that end pole droop out of the way, while the taut wire to the middle pole kept the gate from lying down. Now there was a three-foot opening with just a single wire stretched about knee-high across the gap.

Alex stepped over the low wire to the other side of the fence. He dug into the snow. There were only thin, short strands of grass buried beneath. He lay down and with sweeps of his legs pushed up a fluffy ridge of snow from an area about six feet long and four feet wide, and scraped loose what grass he could. There were four weedstalks standing up close by the fence line. He bunched them with the grasses and set the offering where the horse would have to stretch her neck through the gate opening to reach it. Then, holding the freed gatepost with its wire loop so he could swing it, he hunkered down on his knees and tried to root himself like so much brush in the ridge of snow.

Morena saw the gate sagging, saw the tuft of more food lying beyond. She had watched the man crouch down and stay oddly still in the snow. Her nostrils spread, her ears aimed forward. It fit with nothing she'd ever known. She could neither smell nor hear anything unusual.

She stepped forward. The gate looked open. She felt her hunger and the weather alarm inside her. The loop of old wire on the ground beyond the gate opening meant little.

But the man was there. She saw the unnatural humping of the snow. The man stayed low, and still. Nothing seemed to be watching her. She stopped.

She saw the single low wire in the gap, but no corral. Now she held her head high, her eyes rolled to stare down the long barrel of her face; her ears stayed straight up like rigid horns, cupped forward. Her shoulders shivered with the tenseness of her muscles. She snorted questioningly. Then louder, sharper, demandingly. She got no answer. She turned and trotted away, still in the upper pasture.

Her tail fluttered in a drooping arch, her nose stayed high so she could move and glimpse behind. She might have run into something, but there was nothing there. Nothing chased her. She circled. Nothing chased her. She slowed up. She started back toward the gate. It looked open. She remembered the man. She could still smell him. But what she saw didn't look like him. Her hunger pressed as real as the man; her hunger and the weather alarm inside her. There seemed nothing around. The gate looked open—just a low wire across the gap. She paused, then lunged across it.

The snow burst up beside her. Something swept at her face, clawed down her neck, swiftly struck around her shoulders and bit her!

Alex, up on one foot and one knee, breathless with the joy of having swung the loop over her head, pulled hard to make her stop.

Morena snorted explosively as she tried to buck; she was too stiff to leap high but her hind feet struck back, just past Alex, and hit the heavy brace post. It cracked like a rifle shot behind her. The thing around her neck clamped harder and bit deeper; she tried to spin away, then she saw the shape that had risen beside her, and she ran on the way she was heading. The thing kept pulling and biting.

Alex was hauled bent over forward into a leaping run. He tried to keep hold of the gatepost that kept jolting him nearly into the air, tried to keep even with the horse, and pulling back on her, tried to bring her to a stop, tried to keep from being jerked under the hooves beside him. His foot slipped. He lost his hold and flew face first into the snow, and didn't see the striking hooves that flickered an instant above him.

When he looked up the horse was jumping away downslope. The gatepost was swinging about and beating her sides. He saw it swing down and jam between her hind legs. She fell.

Morena kicked frantically as she lay on the ground, the loop of barbed wire loose and stiff, but clawing at her throat with every movement she made. She saw the shape that was Alex running toward her, but she was too panicked to recognize him as human. She got her front hooves back under her, shoved up-ward, and ran away from him.

But she couldn't run well. The gatepost kept swing-ing at her, and she kept trying to dodge it, and kept getting her legs tangled. She kicked at it but it was tied too close to be hit hard and merely flounced up and swung back.

Alex ran after her.

She fell again.

He spurted ahead with all his strength and breath.

Her jumps had been faster; she got up too soon, and struggled on, and tripped again.

Alex dashed—

She got up, and the gatepost had been broken; its two pieces were hung together only by thin strands of wood, and these were torn apart as she fought the post again. The biggest piece arced off into the snow, and, less awkward now, Morena galloped on farther downslope toward the trees in a lower draw, to rub the rest of her clawing burden off.

Alex gave in and walked. He felt sapped again. With the emergency out of reach, he couldn't make his feet lift up out of the snow anymore, and he had to scuff along through it, and sometimes stumble. The snow was very white and glittering. He was wet and cold from the snow; yet, warm enough, too, from the sun and his running. And he was so angered by the escaped horse that he was almost blind to the wide distances that surrounded him and the frigid cold that was going to start in just another few hours. Almost blind to it. But not quite.

He went on and picked up the broken piece of gatepost as he trudged past. He grabbed again at his hip pocket and found that his knife was still there. He left it there and left his belt loose and ready. But it took him nearly an hour to hike to the lower draw into which the horse had disappeared. He noticed he was having to move only a little north of eastward. If he could catch her, he could just keep going right down the slopes.

He was sure she was still in the draw, hiding and

resting. Maybe she'd gotten the wire and post stub tangled and caught in the brush. Else he'd have to crowd her against some trees. He couldn't let her get out! Most old horses would give up and let you catch them if you got them crowded enough.

Where the hoof scuffs in the snow went into the draw he sat down out of sight, very carefully, to try and figure how to go in after her.

I can't let her get away!

11

Marv Hannum squinted into the fierce, constant glare of the snowy hills and tried to keep his pickup following the hidden trace of the road. In the thick new snow the truck chugged quietly over the round iron bars of the cattle guard that let the road pass gatelessly onto his upper pasture.

He glanced again at the watch strapped to his thick wrist. A quarter past one already. But he couldn't hurry. The barrow pits along either side of the roadway were filled level with snow, and if he slipped off into one even his four-wheel-drive might not help him. So no point in taking chances. Already, with the best of luck, he was going to be late getting to Gene Wall's. The TV reception was better there, and they'd taken to enjoying the pro-football games together every Sunday.

But Debbie had given him no peace about leaving the old mare up in the hills, and the storm hadn't cleared off till late in the morning. He shook his head, the way a bull might, at how little control he had over the things around him. It didn't seem to matter how much he figured or spent. *Even when I quit chasing the old devil,* he thought, his thoughts rumbling on as steady and as tensely as his driving, *and leave her alone, here I am again, because of her.*

It seemed to Marv Hannum that this was the most burdensome animal he'd ever owned. Even in a corral she'd always been hard to catch, for she'd stick her head in a corner or tight against a post, so no noose could drop on her, and aim her tall, mean rump at you, whichever way you approached. And he'd walked many miles the few times he'd forgotten and let the reins slip loose while he was closing a gate, and she'd gone off without him.

Yet he'd never ridden a horse that had more jump getting after cattle, or more calm when you wanted to move slow; never a horse with more sense—self-defense, he guessed it was—when roped to a critter or when angling around badger holes and washouts, or field ice.

So for twenty years he'd used her and been glad of her beneath the saddle, and swore at her in between, till she'd grown too short-winded, and too stiff and apt to stumble. Then he and Debbie had given a party, at the end of which everyone had gone over to the corrals, and they'd sprinkled a glass of expensive whisky over Morena's bony withers, and turned her out to peaceful retirement. At the time it had seemed like an act of noble kindness.

Now it seemed like bad management. Alive and in the sale barn, the old mare would be worth ninety dollars. He could buy several small useful things for ninety dollars. And if he could coax her into the back of the truck, that's where she'd go.

He didn't especially want to sell her for dog food, but he figured he was too honest to sell her for a kid's horse. No kid could catch her, or use her.

In fact it might be kindest—and simplest—if he just used the rifle riding in its clamps behind his head. That way she wouldn't have to suffer from old teeth and old bones, and he'd have his Sunday free.

If he couldn't get her in the truck right away, that idea had its appeal. The coyotes would quickly tear away the mark of the bullet. He'd just keep reminding Debbie that she'd died wild and happy. In fact, that might be easier than arguing her past Debbie to the sale ring. That'd probably cost more than ninety dollars in time and hard feelings.

Marv Hannum stopped a moment to set the rifle down in the seat beside him, then he started the pickup puttering slowly along again as he tried to watch the roadway, and tried to keep watching the distance, too. It was a darn shame it'd come to this, but every animal got old sometime.

He looked up toward the timbered hollow where the Boy Scouts had been planning to camp for the weekend. He suddenly wondered if he'd been right figuring they'd get out okay by themselves. He hadn't wanted to go warn them, for fear the storm wouldn't show after all. He'd figured they had their own radios. Now he didn't see any camp smoke, or any other signs, and was not surprised they'd gotten down all right.

The glare of the sun on the snow was tiring. He stopped the pickup, took his binoculars and stood up outside to scan about. It was warm outside, warm enough that the snow was starting to be wet and melt-ish. Marv Hannum shook his head at the craziness of plains country: storm at night, summer at noon, and bitter freeze sure to come under a clear sky at night. Dampness, and the graze all covered, then freeze.

"If this doesn't kill her, nothing will," he muttered. It seemed to him that if she'd survived the storm she'd be out on the opens trying to paw for food.

He aimed his glasses once toward the blank campground, then slowly down across the slopes—and abruptly he stiffened, and snorted sharply with disgust. He could see a part of the distant fence line, and in it the obviously sagging gate.

"She's busted through it!" he growled. "She's probably busting into the steer lot right now. She'll be home before I will."

Marv Hannum angrily got back in his pickup. A little recklessly he gunned it forward and back, forward and back, working to keep it on the roadway and yet get it turned around. Then still hauling the bales of hay he'd brought to drop if he couldn't find the horse, and not bothering to go down and swing the gate wide as he'd planned, he headed back home. Next he'd have to go check the west gate to the steer lot. He glanced again at his watch and swore and wished he were already down at Gene Wall's.

12

ALEX SPRUNG OPEN HIS EYES AND SAT UP SWIFTLY.
He could tell he'd been asleep. But as he looked about
his alarm faded. The sun was still bright, the shadows
still narrow. A light west wind was up, but the air
was still warm. He'd caught himself in time.

The sharp edge was off his weariness, and he felt
encouraged.

But time was passing. He scooped a handful of
clean, white snow into his mouth to hold down his
hunger. He began to move toward the bottom of the
draw very slowly in the muffling quiet of the snow.
He followed the scuff trail, trying to guess where it
might lead, trying to figure how to catch the horse.

He saw her—the dark bulk in front of a clump of
young aspens that were leafless and winter-scrawny.
The trees were like a sprouted fence. She must've

simply got there and stopped. If he could keep her pressed there, keep her from dodging back and around them—

Alex kept stepping forward, very gently; he kept his arms out at his side, fencelike, hoping he was bluffing at her just right: just enough to mean business, not enough to startle— He kept stepping, waiting for her to see him, and for whatever would happen then.

He sucked in with a warm flood of pleasure. He realized she was caught. The wire loop and the broken gatepost tied about her neck had tangled with a limb.

Alex felt like the King of the Hills on his way to be crowned. Lost, unarmed, desperate, he had captured a horse—or nearly. He kept going very slowly, a little nervously; nothing must happen now. He started to go beside her. She turned her hindquarters toward him.

Whichever side he went to, she swung her rump end toward him; the tall hind legs bent and stomped heavily and awkwardly, but sidestepped quickly through the deep snow. When she moved, the wire barbs bit her, so with each movement her shoulders and neck lurched, too; and with one jolt the branch that held her cracked, but didn't separate. Alex saw that it was too late to go around and try to push through the trees in front of her; if she jumped backward she might pull free and wheel away.

He tugged his belt loose and ready in his hands and tried again to slip in, uncrushed, between her side and the trees. He had to get a hold of her neck. It was the only way he could hold her.

Then something else caught his attention from behind him. He paused, listening uncertainly, almost on tiptoe. It came again, dim but familiar and clear in the quiet air of the draw: the distant gunning sound of a motor.

Alex turned and went scrambling back up the draw's bank. There, on top, he looked, squinting, across all the gleaming snow, and saw nothing, except suddenly a flash of light, then another: the magnified hit of sun on glass.

He couldn't hear the motor anymore. But like a tiny red bug in the distant snow he saw a pickup moving, way upslope beyond the broken gate and the draws he'd left behind. The pickup must be on the roadway. It was angling away to one side, southward. Alex started to run and call after it, but one jump and one shout told him how useless that was. The pickup kept going away.

But Alex didn't worry. He felt great. The pressure was really off. They were out looking for him, and they would find him. Only he'd found the horse first. There would be more than one pickup, and he'd be ready and mounted and in good shape for the next one.

Feeling calm and free of care and ever bolder, he

went back down toward the horse. He walked straight toward her and slapped her hard on the rump with the buckle end of his belt. She kicked, jumped, and jerked harder as the barbs of the wire bit her neck. The aspen limb split apart and fell in front of her. Immediately she heaved back from it, and when the limb dragged in the snow the barbs scraped toward its pull; she stopped again in a moment's shivering nervousness. In that moment Alex strode alongside her. He grabbed her mane with one hand, and the wire's gatepost with the other. "Whoa, now," he ordered.

Morena felt the man's grip on her mane. She was used to giving in to such a grip. She heard the confidence in his voice. It promised relief from the frightening pains around her neck.

Holding onto her with one hand then the other, Alex worked the belt over her neck and buckled it closed. Then, hanging onto the belt and forcing himself to patience, he worked the wire loose from its tangles with the coarse and heavy hair of her mane, and untwisted it from the post and freed her from the whole contraption.

Then, still holding her by the belt, he tried to look at her mouth.

The unnatural, creeping fingers were more extra nervousness than Morena could bear. She threw her head high and tried to jerk away.

Alex held on, but decided not to press his luck.

He hadn't seen the edges of her teeth, but by his glimpse of how the bottom ones leaned forward he felt assured she was old. She wouldn't pitch with him.

"Whoa, now," he repeated. "I won't steal your teeth. All I want to do now is get on you."

13

MORENA KNEW WHAT THE MAN WAS TRYING TO DO. She'd been trained always to turn toward the man mounting her, which helped a person with his foot in a stirrup to swing up. She moved quickly every time the man stretched toward her.

That opened the gap between the hairy ribs and the log he was standing on, and, every time, Alex dropped beside her with his feet in the snow. For the first few tries it was funny; then Alex remembered again that time was passing, any moment someone on horseback or in a big snow tractor might find him. He wanted to find *them*. His weariness showed through. He couldn't control his impatience. He shouted and punched at the horse to make her stand still.

Morena felt the punches; they didn't hurt much,

but they were bothersome. It was the shouting that made her more nervous and frightened again. She tried to jerk away. The man held on. He tried to pull her another way, but she didn't trust him, and moved to face him, so as not to expose her side. Besides, she'd been trained as a roping horse by men who'd pulled on her and kept after her to pull back and keep the strain taut.

When he couldn't get her to go toward another fallen tree, Alex decided to work her toward the draw's bank, where he could stand on higher ground. He kept calm again and spoke kind words to her, and slowly put up his hand, patted her on the neck and scratched her ears, and gently got her moving toward the bank.

To Morena, it was the way toward the haystacks. When they reached the bank, she immediately started up it, plunging forward with the same uphill hurry most horses have.

Alex, in spite of himself, went half dragged, half bounding uphill beside her. It was the only way to hold onto her. In no time at all he was at the top, panting heavily. He looked around for any searchers; and though he didn't see any, he felt himself grow very hurried. Right away he grasped the belt in his left hand; the belt was tight around the middle of her neck. With his right hand level with his own hair he took hold of her mane, leaped up, and tried to swing himself to her shoulders. The horse turned toward

him. She made his knees whip in against the side of her withers, but not over them; he dropped back on the snow. He tried again; almost, he almost made it; he was zeroing in on it; he just needed to swing his right leg out further when he started to jump, then whip it around higher, and he'd get it over her back.

Morena was tired of getting kicked in the ribs. She didn't know what was going to happen to her next. When the man started to leap again, she turned toward him in a hurry.

Alex was nearly flung loose. He struck against her whole side with his arms and legs stretched straight out as if he were flying, then he swung downward, his boot toes jamming in the snow, his arms locked above him hanging onto the belt and mane, the rest of his body swaying awkwardly in between. Morena endured his grip. He pulled his legs back under him. *"Hold on,* will you," he grunted. He got his breath and tried again.

She'd gotten her neck jerked. She turned even quicker.

Alex just barely hung on.

Her neck was yanked again by his weight falling, so now she just kept turning.

"All right, all right," he kept dancing around in front of her as she kept circling; he kept running a big circle in long jumps in order to hang on. "All right!" He finally got her stopped. But he was shaking, nervous. He was angry again, underneath, but he didn't have time for it. Time was passing. He had to get going. He had to use his head. He ought to get closer to the road.

"Let's walk a bit," he puffed, "and get you calmed down." Maybe back up at that fence—

She planted her feet against the pressure and would not go at all back toward those higher, food-less hills.

Alex heaved in his breathing. He didn't want to give up. Not yet. One more try. There was another draw a little further downslope, and maybe a better place to get mounted. He turned her around. "All right. Come on. This way," he coaxed.

Morena understood his tone and did not trust it. But he was pulling her toward the haystacks, so she walked along beside him.

14

WALKING WAS SLOW WORK. THE WORLD WAS HUGE when you could move just a step at a time. Alex tried to think what the world had seemed like, long ago, when nobody could ever move any faster than their own two feet could carry them. He tried to think about how long the hills and slopes and draws, and the small gullies in them, had been then, and what sort of creatures had passed by, doing what? hunting what? *thinking* what? He tried to feel himself cave-man strong, stomping up behind Milt Toppen and telling him, 'You can't leave me behind. I got home anyway.' He tried to imagine the fun of riding all the way into town, up to the walk of his house, saying, 'Don't worry, Mom and Dad. I got through.' He tried to see himself walking among his friends, the only one who'd proved he didn't have to ride home in a hot, stinking bus. He tried to figure out other expeditions he might plan.

He tried to think, and he tried to imagine. But the thin grass had caught enough snow that he still had to slog, or else lift each foot straight up for every step. He could make good snowballs because the snow had softened in the sun and clung to his boots in heavy, breakaway clods, so that he started stumbling from them as much as the horse. The sapped, rubbery tiredness came back in his legs and ached sharper when he tried to fight it, making it harder to concentrate on other things.

Yet he tried to joke about it. "What we need is some *real* clodhoppers," he said aloud.

He said, "If I could just get these clods built high enough under me, I'd step right onto you. I'll bet that'd tickle your backbone."

Words. Words were thin. He began looking more and more often up the long slopes behind him, and he searched the bright, empty sky for airplanes and began to grow impatient with the searchers for not being there, for not giving him some assurance. And he grew more impatient to reach the draw and get mounted before anyone saw him. He gripped harder on the belt around the horse's neck and wanted to twist it tight till she'd have to kneel down and let him on, but he didn't have a tenth the strength it would take.

So he started to sing. The music-rhythm could

make walking easier, make the world seem smaller. For a joke, too, he sang, "Rolling home, rolling home, as we go rolling, rolling—"

The extra air he breathed in awakened the hunger deep in his chest. It swelled up, clawing inside him like a trapped rat. He stopped and scooped up some more snow. It burned down his throat like acid. He began to feel like vomiting again. He fought it off. He fought his legs through the snow. His head felt odd, full of sickness and weariness and glare; the slightest stumble made him dizzy, and aching, and angry. "Dirty deserters," he growled. "And you: you lousy horse!" He didn't try to sing or joke again, or even think. One thought was enough; it was easiest just to fight ahead, packing and armoring his thoughts into one simple solidly angry thought toward every-thing. He looked back and guessed he'd already had to tramp three miles from that gate. At least it was eastward and down.

When they reached the new draw, he found it was a wider, deeper draw than the others, wider and deeper than it had looked to be, and its banks were steep. In the bottom were a good many trees and bushes and deadfalls, and their shadows had started to spread darkly across one another. The whole bot-tom looked dark and jungle-like, a place where big bears might den.

Alex grew angry at the bothersome possibility of bears and drove it from his mind. He wanted to get the horse hemmed in and mounted, and he was going to go down.

But the horse would not go down. She did not want to go into such deep snow and bramble. He pulled on the belt, and she pulled back. His only thought and feeling was anger. He swung at the belt hard, this way and that. She jerked back, pulling him along. He let loose of the belt and flew at her. One hand clamped her mane, the other clawed a bare fingering grip over the high bony knob of her withers, and his legs leaped upward, slamming and digging against her ribs and shoulders for something to hold and push against; he snarled in a complete fury, more like a wildcat than a man as he tried to scale her.

He was too tight against her to be kicked. Morena might have bitten him, but in fright she bolted; she ran with her head high and eyes rolled back to watch him.

Beyond fear, Alex clung to the wall of ribs that was suddenly leaping and jolting. *He'd ride her this way. He'd ride her wherever.* He knew it the moment she stumbled; still in a fierce rage he tried to use the sudden slump and pause that followed to lurch himself higher on her back, and he felt her give to the pull of his weight. Then he felt part of her drop away, and the whole world turning. An instant's glimpse of the vast open draw beneath him startled his senses, and in the instant he pushed himself loose and struck on his side in the snow, knowing more than seeing that the big horse was skidding down right behind him. He tried to drive himself faster than the fall. He plowed and rolled and dove with the vague familiar feeling of doing it before. There was a mass of dead-falls black at the bottom right ahead, and he struggled to dodge and shield himself as he flung into the snow among them and heard the horse strike next to him with a terrible *thunk!*

He stirred for an anxious moment, then knew he was okay, and in a moment more that the horse was down. He fought his way back out to get on top of her.

But there was no hurry. The mare had reached the bottom on her right side, feet first. The two slender legs on that side had slid beneath a thick, dead limb. The solid impact of her chest had apparently rolled the limb upward; now it had settled back, pressing the thigh of the right hind leg against the ground. And there was no way she could move it.

Now it was Morena who lost control. In wild panic she flailed and flailed with her free legs, snapping off arm-thick branches, hammering the solid wood loudly. She kept throwing her head upwards again and again, though each time her head, neck, and shoulders just strained to the point of weakness, and then whipped heavily, with an awful thud, back against the ground.

Alex stood by, helpless for a moment, awed and made small by the horse's violence and the limb's

solid resistance, all of it so far beyond his own powers. He saw blood trickling from scrapes on the pinned leg, and from new cuts on the striking legs. Finally he went to the limb, out of range of the hooves, and pushed on it. It weighed hundreds of pounds. He might as well have pushed on the earth itself. There was nothing he could do but go after help for himself and the horse.

He climbed, with difficulty, back up the scraped embankment, and at the top looked about again for the searchers.

The bright sky was still clear, the gleaming snow still spread out across the long empty slopes. It seemed a long, exhausting way back up to the draws he had left; the distant fence line was noticeable now only because of a threadlike shadow of the snow drifted along it, and the tiny, dark slivers that were the brace posts. But there was nothing else to do but get back to the road.

He wished again for matches, just to build a signal fire. So they would come to him. Wishes were pointless.

And it occurred to Alex as he started trudging that even this was pointless, that if they were looking for him there *would* be planes in the sky; by now there would be more than one truck. They would've started at the campground and fanned out. He would have heard them shouting or shooting; he would see them, right now, on the slopes.

It hit him as sharply as the remembered glare from the windshield that the pickup had come not for him, but for the horse.

He stopped still, a hot flush rushed to his face, and he twisted with the agony of his own stupidity. He should've known no one would leave a horse out alone with snow covering the grass. He should've known someone would come to feed it. And they'd seen the open gate—they must've seen it—and figured the horse was gone. They probably just dropped some hay!

He tried to throw off the deadening shock of having muffed his chance. And the returning misery that somehow there was no search. Somehow, they weren't looking for him.

But, he thought, they might look for the horse down lower. There must be other gates, a feed bunker, some place else that they'd leave hay, maybe for other animals. Maybe with all the snow they hadn't gotten there yet.

Alex turned and in a hurrying panic began to run downslope. He looked back over his shoulder at the sun. How much time did he have, how much time till dark? He was too frightened to really stop and tell. He had to get downslope. That's where a ranch, a feed yard, anything, would be. It was his only chance. The memory of the red pickup spurred him. He had to get downslope, to run into something downslope.

Then he stopped. The pastures were big. He might miss them. The horse knew the way. She must. He needed the horse. But she was pinned down. He couldn't get her loose. He had to get going while he could. He was tired. He had to save what strength he could.

She'd die, pinned down like that all night. What'd he care? He had to get going. She didn't have to have been so spooky. But he'd been stupid, too. The muffled thumping and pounding sounds he could still hear made an echo of the pounding of his heart and the thumping of the fear inside him. He tried to pull away from it, but couldn't. He went back to the edge of the draw. He looked down, and then he looked at the broad slopes running to empty horizons everywhere around him, and he realized that he wasn't too weak to get her free, for if he was then the best he could hope for was hands and feet and ears frozen to blackness and lost by morning. Most likely he would be dead, period.

15

"I THINK YOU CAN TURN THE HEAT DOWN," HIS mother said. "The sunlight through these closed windows is warm enough."

"It's not the sun's *light*." His father grinned. "Light waves are short and pass through the glass, but you can't feel them. It's the long waves sent back from everything inside here, that can't get through the glass so well, that you feel as heat. If you'll come to my general science classes next month, you'll understand that."

"I'm content just to feel it." She smiled. "What I don't understand is why hotels and stores have to be so overheated. They make the weather seem twice as cold when you go out. It was that way everywhere I went."

In spite of his sunglasses, his father was squinting

uncomfortably against the glare of snow-white land, and sitting somewhat on edge to keep the car moving steadily along the slippery and drifted highway.

"You're not supposed to be comfortable at conventions," he said. "They're supposed to seem like work." Carefully he moved a hand free of the steering wheel and pushed the sliding knob to lower the heat. "As slow as we have to go, we'll be turning it back up strong before we even get to Alder."

His mother said, "It's Emma who's been doing the work, I'll bet. With Alex and Dale loose in her house all day—" She paused. "You're sure there's no chance they could've gotten stuck on that mountain?"

He laughed. "Milt Toppen likes his comfort too much. I'll bet those kids got yanked out of there even before dark last night."

"It would be nice to be sure," she said.

"What would you do if they were stuck?" he said.

"What do you mean?"

"I mean if they were snowed in up there, starving and freezing. You'd hurry back as fast as you could. And that's what we're doing. Might as well relax and enjoy the trip. They're not freezing or starving. They're keeping Emma and Nick warmed and stirred, that's what they're doing."

"I think we ought to stop and call at our next chance."

"What for?"

"At least we could give some moral support."

"That wouldn't help much. And worse," he smiled, "it might start them feeling sorry for themselves."

"Oh, I don't think that's true," she said lightly. "But I suppose it would be silly; we're late enough already. Alex and Dale actually get along together rather nicely." She stretched a little where she sat, straining up against the grip of the seat belt, and then relaxed as the car kept moving slowly onward.

In California, men sweating in brightly colored uniforms chased each other and knocked each other down on the smooth green grass under a warm, high sun. From the sidelines the crowds of people yelled and the red lights on television cameras winked.

Eastward over the great mountains, where the sun was settling toward the peaks, and on beyond the crests of the Finger Hills, and down further in the town of Belle Ore, Milt Toppen lay on the living room rug, his head propped against the soft cushion on his sofa, and in perfect comfort he watched the game. His wife, coming into the room softly, as she always did, noticed the knapsack stacked by the front door hallway.

"Oh, who's is it?" she asked. "I guess Vic Rabel's."

"Alex Jaynes'," he said.

"Why, of course. You said the poor kid was sick. How is he now? Did you call his grandfolks?"

"No, the game was starting just as I got in from fixing up that bus. I'll call when it's over."

Dale Logelin, with closed schoolbooks piled at his feet, sat with his father in their house and watched the game.

In the Walls' ranch house, Debbie Hannum and Wilma Walls chatted in the kitchen. Marv and Gene, with sandwiches and drinks piled on the card table just behind them, with their boots pulled off and the chairs low and soft beneath them, rested their elbows on the thick arm cushions and relaxed and watched the game.

16

"WHY AREN'T THEY LOOKING FOR ME, HORSE?" HE cried. He had come back down into the draw, and the horse, for all her heavy pounding, was still held down by the stiff, dead weight of the limb. He had sat down just to rest and plan a moment, but his body wanted only to sag completely into sleep; his hunger tore at him with a harsh, speechless loneliness. He heard the throatless whine of the light breeze moving steadily through the treetops, and he became aware of some tiny whistling cheeps behind him. He turned and saw a flutter of chickadees moving hop-hop in and about some cedars. Hop-hop. *Chitter chitter, chick-a-dee-dee-dee.* Just as if nothing were wrong. Just as if the air in the draw wasn't already noticeably cooler, cold enough to chap his hands again. Hop-hop. Little half-handfuls of feathers. They were warm enough. They would be alive tomorrow. For one instant Alex had a wonderful dream of surviving draped deeply in chickadee feathers—from several thousand birds. It was impossible. A short while before he would have thrown a stick at them, but now his anger was spent and meaningless. There was only a rush of tears that, in spite of himself, burst out and flooded down his cheeks.

"Where are they?" he cried out loudly. "Where's Milt Toppen? Or Mr. Mittleton—or Mom and Dad? Why don't they come?"

The chickadees had hushed. But the horse gave another stuttering squeal and grunted heavily as she squirmed and struck her hooves at the tree, raised and then *thomp*ed her head back against the ground.

"You stupid ass!" he screeched, leaping up. "If you weren't such a lousy, stinking smear we could —ah—"

He ended with a gasp. Something dark, and silent, like a huge wing, had passed over him. The air was suddenly colder. For a moment he stood stiff in the mixture of terror and self-misery that must hold a mouse rigid even when it sees the swooping owl. He stood in complete shadow. The sun had gone below the tops of the cedar trees at the head of the draw.

He wanted to quit. He wanted to lie down and relax, just close his eyes and go to sleep and surrender. They weren't looking for him anyway.

The horse banged into another spasm of helpless

effort. If she were loose they could move. He couldn't resist that thought. He went closer. Then for the first time he saw the limb not as something blocking his urgent hurry, but as merely a problem in general science. Everything, his father had told him, was just a question of science. When the sun went, the snowy ground would radiate back the little bit of heat it had gathered during the day. Without clouds to hold it in, the heat would rapidly rise through the air toward the stars. The mercury in the thermometers would contract down the scales. The blood vessels in his own body would contract, and he would have to discover how to find shelter. Or in a few hours his nerves and flesh would be growing more and more numb, and white, at first. Soon he would be in death, perhaps before the gangrene blackness started; and the coyotes, at least, would come searching for him and keep the draw clean. Calmly, he admitted that he was going to be part of an interesting experiment, either way.

So he looked and looked and convinced himself that what faced him was really as simple as it seemed. He couldn't understand why it had frightened him off so before. The right hind leg simply had to be pulled back uphill, less than a yard, or the limb shifted the other way or raised just a little; and she could drag herself free. If the mare would just put her loose hooves against the limb and push—braced as she was against the draw's bank—she'd probably be strong enough to move it herself. But she only pawed out trying to get all her hooves immediately under her. No science to it at all, wasting all that energy.

Suddenly it occurred to Alex that the only reason he wanted to move was to reach warmth, but that there was more warmth already inside him and that horse than there was anywhere for miles around. In science, his father had said, you have to keep an open mind. He didn't have to *ride* a horse. Carefully Alex looked at the horse, considering how he might cut her open, to trap the blood, and then get the fat and meat that was there. Raw, but it would give him heat energy inside him. Then he could cover her with boughs and crawl inside, trapping his own body heat completely. He could see himself surviving fine. But it was risky: a new storm might come. All the miles would still be there. And there was time yet for that; she'd be better for him alive.

Calmly. Saying, "Easy now," in a soothing way, Alex moved to the front of her and tried to set her forelegs the right way to push on the limb. They were unbelievably heavy, and she jerked them away and groaned terrifyingly loud right at his ears as she tried to get herself straight up again.

Alex stayed calm. The task was plain. "Easy now," he coaxed. "Do it my way, girl. We'll get you out."

Morena had never pushed on limbs before in her life. She was terrified at being pinned down and unable to run. She could feel the air getting colder. Her caught leg pinched and hurt. She didn't know what the man was trying to do. She struck at him. She would strike any danger.

Alex jumped back. Calmly. This part of this experiment would have to be altered. He'd have to use his own leverage. You didn't have to be a horse, or well-fed, or even looked-for, to use the laws of leverage. He needed just a rock or log for a fulcrum and a long stout pole to pry with.

There were sure to be plenty about. Of course the snow had drifted in and covered them. The wood that was stout enough and still standing was too stout for him to break down. He had to be patient. As he kicked and scuffed about, he noticed that the sunlight above him was taking more and more of a slant. Soon it would separate into colors—filtration caused by dust and moisture in the atmosphere. He knew his cheeks were tingling with cold and once more he began having to put his fingers in his pockets to get them warm. He saw the horse watching him with rolled eyes, half white. Her breath was pumping her ribby sides up and down. Sprawled against the snowy ground, she looked thin and scrawny.

But the hide was still windproof and waterproof, Alex thought. Huddled in it, he might get through till morning. He'd have to stab her somewhere in the neck to kill her; she would throw her head around and the muscles would be tough. Then he'd have to cut open a doorlike flap in her belly. He'd probably have to get the knife up between her ribs to open air holes. There was work there, too. There was time yet, he thought.

He gradually found some broken branches he could stack as a fulcrum, and he worked carefully to get them in position. He didn't want to accidently stand where that free hind leg could thrash at him.

Finding a prying pole took longer. In general science, you just got a piece of polished wood off the counter. In general science, Leverage and Weather and Forests were all in separate chapters. Here it was all mixed together, and he was just something inside it. He kept tromping about until he found a four-inch-thick sapling that had been smashed down by the fall of a large cedar. Like everything else it wasn't a clean break. He cradled it up against his chest and staggered with it forward and back, till he'd tortured it from its stump. His hands were raw and aching again; his fingers had gotten so thick and stiff again he couldn't feel what he held and he dropped it twice; the hard pressure of dragging the wood started his toes aching with cold again. The snow was thick, and the wood was heavy; it dragged deep and stuck. Exhaustion and breathlessness made him rest. Overhead rays of sunset had begun to gleam in rich gold across the sky. Time was running short.

Finally he dragged his sapling pole onto his fulcrum and got the short end jammed to the bottom of the limb. At the long end he began to shove downward; he strained downward with his shoulders and thighs. His fingers on the bark burned with cold beneath his pressure. The pole dipped downward, a little, a little more. He kept straining. At the other end the limb was tilting upward. The horse's leg was loose, but she didn't move.

"Move," he puffed at her. She lay still. *"Move!"* She didn't and his breath gave out, and he had to let off; the limb settled back. Then she moved, fighting and striking helplessly all over again.

He tried again. This time as the limb raised, she moved, too. She tried to thrust herself straight upward, and hit the limb, shaking it off the pole. Alex's end flew downward beneath his pressure, and he belly-flopped across it on the ground. His breath was punched out of him. He fought desperately to get back on his feet before she got away. It took him almost a minute. She was still beneath the limb. His fingers had come out of the freezing snow so stiff it was a while more before he could move them. Over him, he saw orange beginning to streak with the gold. His life was narrowing. If this prying didn't work soon, he'd have to kill her and crawl inside her and wait, for whatever happened. He reached behind to feel his knife for assurance, and it was still there. Tumbling fall and all, it was still there! But he'd wait ten minutes or so for that yet. He'd rather have her warm and rideable. You never should rush an experiment.

17

"Move!—Dammit!—"

Unrushed, but steadily, red leaked out from the orange in the sky and spread and formed streaks of its own. Unrushed, but steadily, pale greens and blues washed in from the west and deepened and fanned.

"Dammit!—Do it right!—"

Unrushed, but steadily, the sky seemed almost to laugh, a clownish face peering down, smeared with glowing colors. Unrushed, but steadily, red and yellows thinned and weakened; the greens shrank upward deep into blues.

"Please!—Move!—Please!"

Unrushed, but steadily, the blues turned to rich purple, then faltered, and grew dull. The sky was gray. A few tiny stars appeared, glittering clearly.

But Alex didn't reach for his knife. "Just one more

time," he grunted, and grunted again, and finally she reacted in the right way, she cramped the trapped leg away from the lifted limb and dragged herself free and heaved shakily up on her hooves. He stumbled awkwardly toward her, on cold feet. She was too stiffened to get away. She didn't try. He caught her and stood with his arm hooked through the belt around her neck and pressed his paining fingers into the warmth beneath her mane. For his feet there was no relief but to stamp them up and down. His shoulders kept wanting to shiver, but that was as much from the relief of getting her loose as from the cold. His thoughts soared with the *un*-panicky feeling that he was winning. He was going to make it!

Morena stood holding one hind leg off the ground; not the leg that was pinned, but the other, the left one. She accepted the man's steady hold around her neck. She was used to that kind of control. Her energies had been drained for the moment. It was one more of those rare moments that she felt a man's presence as soothing.

Alex was amazed at how untired and unsleepy he felt. His head worked sharp and clear. He saw there was no point in getting on her now: she couldn't carry him up the embankment, and the brush surrounding them was too thick to ride through. He'd have to mount when he got in the open—but, at last, he knew how. So first he led her slowly about the deep twilight in the hollow of the draw's bottom; it was all a cold stillness of snow grays and brush blacks. She limped, favoring a hind foot.

"Got yourself pinched, did you?" he said gently. "It'll loosen up with walking," he promised. He moved around till he found a long, thin forked branch he could break off. Then he broke off an arm of the branch so that he had a piece of wood shaped like a long checkmark. With the hook of the check through the belt he could reach her tail and still have hold of her.

He began slicing off long strands of hair. Several times he had to stop and warm his fingers against her body; he wished he knew how to warm his toes, too. He twisted strands of tail hair into long bunches that he tied into loops, one through the other, making a daisy-chain. When he got ready to tie an end loop to a knot in her mane, he'd have a ladder to climb on with.

He put the loops inside his shirt so the brush wouldn't snag them, and began trying to get up on open pasture. "Come on, old girl," he said.

The light breeze greeted them there; light, but singeing with chill. Alex connected his horsehair chain, abandoned his checkmark stick, and while she kept turning toward him, he climbed up and aboard.

"Atta girl. Atta girl," he murmured to her when he was seated. He had to lean way forward on her neck to keep hold of the belt, so he undid the top loop of tail hair and tied it to the belt. Now he had a rein, all of one he should need. It was simple. He couldn't understand why he hadn't thought of it before. All her extra strength and speed was now his, and it felt tremendous.

He lightly urged her into motion, letting her pick the way. She seemed ready to head toward someplace, probably to shelter. The earth was aglow with snowlight. The sky was black and glittering with stars. The directions were clear. She was heading east, toward the highway. She kept limping, still favoring the hind foot. "It'll get warmed up and feeling better," he encouraged her. "The best thing's to keep it moving—old friend."

Low in front of him he saw a star moving. Then another. In fact, there were three of them, spaced out and moving, very slowly; and one more moving the other way. Headlights, he recognized. He was seeing the highway, maybe not much more than twenty miles, direct from where he was.

Her bony spine was gouging hard between his hips, but he didn't mind; he clung close to her warm, solid, hairy strength. It was his safety. The prize he'd won. And he knew for sure why it was he hadn't let himself throw up in the bus, or stay shivering close to the roadway, or cut her throat in the draw and crouch down hoping the cold wouldn't find him. He didn't want to have to accept anyone's forgiveness for stinking up their air, or bringing them out in the cold. Because it seemed like a part of you died and was lost, anyway, every time you did that. He wanted to do things on his own, get there on his own. He was as good as the chickadees. As big as the horse. He'd never felt freer and more whole than he did at that moment.

He grinned down at them, those people hunched in their cars, crowded up close to the heaters they needed, and not knowing they were being watched, not knowing what was going on in the rugged world around them. But he was surviving this world they were hurrying to be shielded from, and he was going down to show them.

"They can't desert us, can they, horse. We'll show 'em."

Morena's hind foot pained her if she stepped on it. It didn't bother her if she held it up, but it was difficult to gimp through the snow on three feet, and she had to keep setting it down again and again. She wanted to stop. But the will of a man on her back had always proved irresistibly strong, and she had learned early to obey it. And her hunger urged her on toward the haystacks. But Morena had little pride when other horses were not around, and it would have taken much pride to dull the stabbing in her hind foot, and to soften and freshen the stiff age in her muscles; much pride to make her try to move

smoothly and gamely. She *hobbled*. Eventually she reached another fence line, right at a gateway. The gate was open and she started through, but the rider made her stop.

The fence line offered a hitching post, should he need it, yet Alex just sat, knowing that the limp was getting worse and that he shouldn't ignore it. But he didn't want to get off the horse.

He wondered if she were faking. He knew that if something was caught in her hoof, and stayed there, she could lame up and move too slow to get any-where. The snow beginning to squeak beneath her steps left no doubt that the rigid cold was settling. His feet were numb beneath the grip of his knees against her ribs. His feet would be warmer moving about in the snow than dangling in the air. He might save his hands under her mane but his feet and ears could freeze if he had to ride too long. He knew he ought to get down for awhile anyway. He could get up again easy now.

Slowly, he slid off of her. He gathered his rein of loops loosely in his hand, and shoved his hands in his pocket. He stood hunched and shivering, and not eager to try wrestling with the hoof she was holding up. But he was again suddenly aware of how small each step of his own would be compared to the brit-tle snow-gray world all around him. He didn't know where any shelter was. He'd have to ride, and ride at a trot in order to get anywhere in time. A trot bareback was jolting, but it got you warm. He looked closely at the hind leg she was favoring. He told himself he'd gotten this far, so he was tough enough to handle it. And the tiny headlights slowly moving in the silent distance reminded him of who he was and where he would finally have to go. He wasn't going to have to make any excuses for coming in on a crippled horse.

He tied his rein to the fence's brace post, then stepped back to lay a palm on the bunched up hip above the leg she was favoring. "Easy now, girl," he spoke to her, and heard his jaw only able to mumble again from the cold. But it didn't worry him; it didn't count now. "I gotta see what's here." He let his hand travel smoothly down the leg. It was a risky business picking up some horses' feet. He didn't want to get slammed and broken now. But she was old. "Easy now," he kept talking. "Easy. I bet you've had your hooves picked up and trimmed a thousand times."

He crouched in close beside her, knowing it was safer to be near the start of a kick than near the end of it. He took a deep breath, exhaled another. "Easy girl." He reached down and took hold of the feathering of hair just behind the hoof and tugged it forward and upward a little. He clamped his thighs together and got the front of the hoof resting against the sloping platform on his lap. Then he learned she was used to this, too used to it: she leaned on him, and his feet pained with cold as part of her weight sank through his legs. The underside of the hoof was packed with snow. With one hand he reached his knife, and began to scrape the snow away. Only then did it occur to him that this wasn't the leg that'd been pinned, and he wondered if he was as alert as he thought he was.

He was alert enough to see the splinter of wood emerging from the snow. It was lodged in one of the 'frog hollows'—the grooves around the fleshy T-shaped pad that cushioned the hoof's step. A reward from all that useless banging and kicking about. She was old, and the pad was thin and hard. He tried to dig the splinter out with his finger, but it was wedged and held by snow stamped to water and frozen again. The flesh of his finger began to freeze and tear first. Then his back began to quiver with the strain, and so he couldn't keep his knees from shaking, too, and he had to let go, and straighten up.

He panted, and moved stiffly about, shaking his feet, trying to get some bearable relief from their aching. Then he patted her flank and felt again, old and skinny though she was, how much bigger and solider she was than he.

"Easy again, now, girl," he murmured. "Easy." He ran his hand slowly down the ridge of her leg. Abruptly she jerked up, and he leaped away, and she jumped. For a moment both of them staggered about defensively, as Alex began to understand she hadn't been kicking, but merely lifting her leg for him.

"Easy, girl. Easy." He started again. He crouched down, and tugged, and gritted against the weight she abruptly shifted to him. He was scared of prying and suddenly pricking too deep with the clumsy, broken point of the knife, so he used the back of the blade and sharply struck to break the ice. It was like the tap of a shoer's hammer. A sharp, hard snap; a startling voice without a body or smell or meaning she ever felt sure of. It had always unnerved her. She swiftly drew up her leg and kicked blindly at it.

Alex felt the hoof jerk up past his shoulder, and as he tried to jump aside the leg kicked by him at a glance so hard that he was shoved into running faster than his own legs could move, and he unbalanced into a snowy roll.

The extra dim commotion made Morena more startled, and she kicked and crowhopped about in nervous alarm, still fighting the ghost with the sharp touch and voice. The horsehair holding her to the brace post snapped with the first jump and she moved willy-nilly out on the pasture, then realized she was free and moved on.

Alex tried to follow, at first slow and then running, as best he could in the snow. But she wouldn't let him close, and even on three legs she could go faster than he when she had to. Soon it was hard just to see her in the darkness, even against the dull white sweep of the snow.

Only the stars were clear, and the little lights on the highway, and the squeaking of the snow. The scuffed trail she'd left in the snow was difficult to follow, for the snow broke too softly to shadow well, but he kept finding it, following it.

He put his knife away when the cold ache in one hand told him he still carried it. He wondered why he hadn't fallen on it. He certainly hadn't thought to throw it out of his way. No, he wasn't as alert as he should be. But now he still had it. He wondered why. He didn't want to believe it was luck. If he hadn't stabbed himself just because of luck, he'd have to thank luck for whatever else he ever did. Then he thought of how an eyelid closed automatically when something got near the eye, and he decided he must have, that quick, without knowing it, held the knife flat. He didn't let his thoughts come to the main fact, that now he was without a horse or solid shelter. That thought would end everything, except the icy pains.

He began to wonder if he were in the grip of some Power, or God, like they spoke of in church. That idea made everything seem less threatening, in fact, interesting. He'd just have to keep going to find out how this mysterious Plan would all work out.

The thought of God had made him naturally glance upward. He saw the two Dippers curved in front of him: the horse's trail had turned northward. Yes, the distant headlights were off to his right. It didn't matter. The highway was too far off to reach afoot. The stars told him he'd gotten to ride less than an hour. It must be close to seven o'clock. There would be an hour more at the most, and then he'd begin to feel his feet and hands starting to puff and stiffen and die. He would get very sleepy. They said when you froze to death, you simply got pleasantly drowsy and drowsier.

If he'd turn back south, he might cut across the road from the campground, a lot sooner than he could reach the highway. But there was no one looking for him there anyway. He wasn't angry at them anymore for not being there. They probably had their reasons. He wasn't even angry at the horse; she'd gotten away, and in her place he'd probably have done the same thing. He just wanted to get where he wanted to get, that was all. He began to wonder if she were real, or just a dream, or a ghost leading him on. She seemed to be heading somewhere. East and north. To shelter? Anyway, his feet were a little warmer walking steadily than riding, and the breeze got to him less than when he was on the horse.

It occurred to Alex that if he didn't keep pumping along, the breeze would wipe out the trail ahead of him. But he was getting tired. And sleepy. He couldn't get worried or angry about that, either. He just had to keep going, no faster than was comfortable. Yet he started finding that the harder it was, the harder he kept wanting the going to be. He kept wanting to take and give as much as he could. They'd have a hard time finding him, even if they wanted to. The breeze was wiping out his trail, too. So he kept struggling, stumbling, north and east. He was going to make it on his own. Or become a mystery. And that was the next best thing.

18

DALE LOGELIN STOOD PATIENTLY AMONG THE adults in his family's living room. He enjoyed almost any occasion that was unusual, and especially this one, because his contributions to the conversation seemed to be central and important.

"Now are you sure," Mrs. Jaynes was saying earnestly to him, "that Alex said he just had a sick stomach. His face wasn't hot was it? Did you notice if he looked flushed? I don't suppose anyone there took his temperature, did they?"

"Of course not," Alex's father answered, before Dale could. "It was just a case of too much hot dogs and horseplay. It's part of the Scout manual." Mr. Jaynes laughed.

"He didn't tell anyone he was sick, but me," Dale said quickly, getting himself back in the talk. "We figured we'd keep it secret so as not to worry anyone and make us all go back early. We were going to leave pretty soon anyway, on account of the storm."

"So, since he was feeling sick he decided to go home to Gram's instead of coming here to play. Real tough and sensible," Alex's father said proudly. "Both of you," he added. "And now I think we'd better be getting home. Sounds like it'll take us a couple more hours."

"We'd better phone first to see how he is," Mrs. Jaynes said.

"He's full of Grandma's lemon pie," Mr. Jaynes said. "A great antidote for mulligan. But I suppose you're right. It's after seven already. We should phone, so your worrying family won't be worrying about us. Do you mind—" Dale watched him speak to his own father. "I presume your talking machine works. You did pay your bill last month, didn't you?"

"Oh, yes," Dale's father joked back. "We're apt to pay our bills every once in a while."

Alex's father picked up the phone, and Alex's mother stood impatiently close by, and Dale felt all the adult interest turning away from him. Soon the visitors would be gone, and the quiet, familiar routine of his own family would settle around him; already the pleasant little excitement was as good as done.

"Hello, Gram," he heard Alex's father's voice speaking. "We're just calling to tell you not to worry about us. We're at the Logelins' in Alder. The roads are snow-packed but we're coming through all right. We probably won't be home till after nine. How's Alex?"

"What—!"

There was something about the ring of that last word that laid a sudden, refrigerator-humming silence all through the house. Dale felt the shift of everyone's attention to Alex's father.

Alex's father was looking down at the phone as if the dial had eyes. "Didn't he call you?—" Then Alex's father straightened up. Dale saw that the man's eyes were dark and round and wild-looking. "He's not there!" Alex's father shouted. And every eye in the room glared at Dale.

"Milt," his wife spoke to him, "this camping gear is still in the hallway. Couldn't the Jaynes boy come get it?"

"Oh my gosh. I forgot to call," said Milt Toppen, dropping down his magazine. "I'll bet that boy's worried into his boots," he grinned, "thinking he left everything up in the hills."

He stood and started for the phone, but just as he reached for it, it rang at him. He startled a little, then picked it up: "Hello . . . Who? . . . Doug Jaynes?—Oh, hello, Doug. I know just what you're calling for," he grinned.

"And yep, I know that, too. He went to his grand-

ma's . . . He's not? . . . *They* never saw him?
. . . Why, he told me he was going there, instead
of his friend's in Alder. Say, maybe he went there,
anywa— Oh, you are there . . . Yep, I'm sure he
said it, right as he got on the bus. I *thought* he got
on the bus. Of course, we went down in a hurry, there
was this storm blowin— Yep, I'm *sure* he got in . . .
No, we just let them off in front of the school—
maybe he just went home with one of his friends here.

"No, Doug, I *don't* know. That's Len Mittleton's
job, ain't it? He's the scoutmaster. You call Len, and
he ought to tell you just what boys were there. Over
in some other kid's house is where you'll find him,
I'll bet you . . . Sure . . . Sure . . . You bet.
Glad to help you."

"Dang!" he exclaimed as he hung up. "I forgot to
tell him about the knap—"

He didn't finish because he suddenly realized his
wife was standing right beside him. She was a soft
woman, but her pale eyes looked very wide.

"His father doesn't know where he is?" she said,
strangely.

"No, he—"

"And he's not at his grandma's?"

"No," Milt Toppen said, growing uncomfortable
in front of his wife's staring. "It's like I told Doug.
The kid's gone off to some other kid's—"

"If a twelve-year-old boy suddenly came home
with your son at midnight, unexpectedly, wouldn't

you have called his parents, *or his grandparents,* by now?"

"Why— Why, sure, I—"

"You didn't count them off the bus?"

"No, I was tired— It was Len Mit— Well, why didn't you remind me about it then?"

"Milt Toppen!" Her eyes were very wide and almost bubbling. "You better call Len Mittleton, too."

As much to escape her eyes as for anything, he looked back down to the phone immediately.

"No, wait," she said. "Give his father's call a chance to get through."

"God," he muttered, looking up. "If Len don't know where he is, I'll bet I'll have to go out and ride back up there with them—well, why do you keep looking at me like that?" he yelled at his wife. "I didn't go and get lost!"

19

HE HAD TAKEN HIS KNIFE AGAIN AND SAWED OFF HIS shirttail and wrapped it and his handkerchief around his ears, and then cut the whole lower half of his undershirt in half to stuff in his pockets with his hands. Perhaps it helped. The cold stayed like sharp nails, pinching all over him. There was nothing special to reach for, nothing to grab at that could help him, nothing he might shelter in, no way to drive out the hurt and weariness. His feet were thick and clumsy, he was stumbling constantly; each jolt brought his hands jerking out of hiding in his pockets, and left him weaker.

The stars glittered sharply over him, but his eyes were watering from the icy breeze, so that the bright star in Lyra seemed to dance, and the Big Dipper indeed seemed to be pouring into the Little. He tried to smile at the thought. His lips were cracked and stiff. The stars turned into the eyes of millions of bats, hanging in a black cave. Alex snarled up at them, like a harried badger snarls at the dogs above him, only his jaw scarcely moved.

He wished he *was* a badger, thick with fur, able to dig a den in seconds. He wished he were a mink, an otter, a rabbit. He wanted to let his head droop down to his chest. And close his eyes and sleep. He wanted to sleep in soft, warm fur.

"Snow is great insulation. Snow can keep you warm," Mr. Mittleton had lectured them, at the warm meeting in the school gym. Not this snow. Not if it got hold of you. You needed fur, you needed a sleeping bag, something between you and the snow. Something like a horse.

He tried to laugh. Again what laughter there was, was locked inside him and turning bitter. The snow squeaked shrilly beneath each step.

"If you've got the stars, there's no reason for you ever to get lost," his father had told the Science Club, outside on a warm September night.

He didn't need the stars, he needed shelter! He was being drowned in bad advice! There were no warm directions in the stars, no warm softness in the snow! The cold was dropping on him—

He pitched forward; he fell flat. He quickly kicked and rolled over to get his face and hands out of the crusty snow; he rolled over because he couldn't find

111

the energy to stand back up. He lay still, on his back. It felt so good just to relax and lie still. The stars whirled over him, but he got them to hold still, too.

"You're the Swan, aren't you?" he mumbled to the shape that shone bright among the Milky Way. "I know you. How do you keep your wings held out, for thousands and millions of years? Wouldn't it feel good just to fold them and rest?"

"If I did I'd fall down."

It was like a sound—a voice—!

Alex jerked himself up. It was starting: the freezing, the deadening. The dreaming. He got back on his feet. His feet felt as big and stiff as his boots, his hands were raw and paining from the snow chafing, he was dizzy; he couldn't remember what it was he was looking for. He realized he was on a downslope, and he had to stop and concentrate on adjusting his balance so he wouldn't fall down again. And at last he remembered the snow scuffs and began trying to follow them lower. The snow got deeper. He saw the horse, stopped by another gate, right in the angle of a fence corner.

Morena still held her left hind foot up. It still pained her to stand on it. She'd grown chilled and very tired, and she was shivering. She was hungry. She wanted to get on to the haystacks. She saw the man coming and immediately nosed into the fence corner. She couldn't depend on where she might have to go if she were ridden.

The man moved this way and that behind her. She kept getting her rear legs toward him. She knew he couldn't reach her well that way; here in the open she could duck and swing away from a tossed loop. She'd learned these things well.

The man climbed through the fence. She moved away from it and eyed the gate, with her head canted just off to one side, as if in deep thought. The gate stayed closed. The man climbed back. She didn't want to leave the gate. The man came after her. She plunged around him and put her head back in the corner.

Alex had jumped for her; his feet had dragged in the deep snow. He stood, breathing hard. The horse was still something to grab at, but he stayed exhausted, gasping; the iced air was galling his lungs. He saw that the knot he'd made in her mane had shaken loose; and his ladder was gone from the belt. Now he'd have no way to hold her while he cut more hair. He'd have to catch her first, anyway. He couldn't face the chore of prying loose more frigid wire. "If I could catch you, horse—I'd kill you," he panted, "and I'd eat and sleep—But I don't know if this fence leads anywhere—or just in circles—Maybe it wouldn't work warm enough—Maybe just my feet would freeze—In the morning I couldn't move anyway." Alex felt his voice getting higher, felt it leaping out between breaths, yet he wasn't really sure if he was talking or just thinking he was talking. "Are you

real, horse?—Or a spook?—Where are we, horse?—
I'm too bushed to catch you, horse—But I can follow
—You're heading somewhere—I don't care if it's
shelter or nowhere, horse—I'm coming, too—I'm
getting there, by myself." He shuffled his way to the
gate, slipped it loose and let it fall; and stumbled
back.

Morena saw the gate go down—she knew where
the haystacks were—and the risk of being caught,
of having to carry and travel. She was tired and
chilled. She was tempted and worried. She was lame,
slower than she wanted to be; she started to go forward, but hesitated. She looked here and there. She
waited, eyeing the gateway—her head canted suspi-
ciously off to one side—for some feeling of what
to do.

Alex waited. He began to shiver; his whole body
began shaking and jerking roughly, and his teeth
clattered at the cold like a machine gun faster than
he could control them. He flew back into a misery
and helpless anger. The worst that horse could do
was just stand there. He tried to charge toward her.

Then the horse, or spook, or whatever it was,
moved. Heavily and awkwardly it plowed around
him, and through the gateway, kicking great bursts
through the deep snow. For an instant he'd heard
its insides rattling. Then he watched it bounding
away from him, rising upward, disappearing upward
through a curtain of misty gray night.

With a yowl Alex charged after it, with a sudden excited freshening of spirit—the mystery made it all worth it—he plunged himself forward through the churned up snow. But the air iced his lungs, and his leg muscles could not long respond, and quickly he was just floundering, confused because the snow seemed on a level with his eyes, even though he could feel that it just went to the tops of his shoes. Finally it dawned on him that he was on an upgrade, and that that was what had made the horse seem to fly. He clawed on, and panted, and forced the paining upward push. Shelter or dying, he didn't care. All that mattered was that he find where that horse was going.

He made it to the top and held still, stymied by his own senses that gave him a queer sensation of warmth the moment he got there. It made him pause, even in his breathing. It was thicker than the air, hauntingly familiar; a brushing of sharp, decaying warmth. With a jolt his mind adjusted, remembered. Manure and livestock, that's what he smelled. And as he began to move slowly, peering, down that other side, he began to make out the dark and lumpish shapes of cattle.

20

He heard the soft hissing of their breathing, the dull thudding as a few took alarm. But they didn't move off far. He could sense the warmth of their bodies more strongly, see the warm steam rising from their nostrils, and from their droppings. He forgot about the horse, right away he was moving about, from one hope to another, gingerly, hand stretched out, like a beggar.

"Whoa, cow. Whoa, fella," he pleaded, mumbling. If they'd just lie still; if they'd just let him crowd in among them.

"Whoa, critter. Lie still. Please lie still."

If one would just lie still, just one steer let him curl against him.

One by one, group by group, they got up as he came close. He stopped, kept his hand stretched out in the cold for them to investigate. Some stretched their necks and heads to meet him; they sniffed curiously, puzzledly, amazedly, but the moment he moved a step closer they humped up and swung away.

One dropped fresh manure in a steaming heap in front of him. He knelt beside it. Ground-up and acidified grass it was, and it was warm and soothing for a few moments to his stiff, raw fingers. There was enough heat in their bodies to heat barns. He could see dark, melted splotches in the snow where they had lain. He saw another darkness, a long flat curve of it, like a highway, through the splotches. He found it was hay, trampled hay. This was a feeding area. Someone had brought hay. They'd be back tomorrow. Tomorrow. He couldn't last until tomorrow. They'd find him dead in a feedlot, surrounded by a hundred furnaces he wasn't good enough to catch. There wouldn't even be any mystery to it.

He started to look for the horse. The horse was gone. Escaped. She'd mingled her trail on the packed ground. How much circling would it take to find it again? Had she backtrailed? Was she real? He hadn't touched any one of the cattle. Was anything real— anymore?

Not even the sudden cries sounded real, the vibrating shrieks that burst out in the night like the wails of mountain lions, or wildcats, but had to be horses; horses whinnying at each other. Just horses, loose horses? Or was the ranch nearby?

Where had the sounds come from?

North. He guessed north. He'd keep on to the north.

Alex scuffed across the hay, on over more melted splotches, straight among more dopily dodging cattle, into untrampled snow. Northward, he started to meet the next rise. The feeling was gone from his feet. He couldn't tell his feet from his boots. There were just two dead weights dragging back at him. His leg muscles were knotting up, aching and trying to quit at the beginning of every move. He fought them, he made his legs push his feet up into the snow, then drag them on; his hands slapped into the snow, snagging at brush holds they were too stiff to grasp. His chest kept heaving, then shrinking and coughing at the bite of the sharp air in his throat and lungs.

When he got on the crest, he stood covered with stars. His head was throbbing as he tried to look down, tried and tried to stare down at the emptiness of more hills that he surely might see. He looked: more timber, bottom timber, another draw, steep and tall here but shallower across. There was a shadowy furrow in the snow across that looked like part of a road. And from the dark timber, square dark corners were poking out against the dim gray slopes beyond.

He started immediately down the steep slope beneath him, clumsily striding and stumbling, then skiing on his side, his stomach, the seat of his pants. He got to his feet on leveler ground and kept going, the snow deepening again as he got lower. He began to see amid the timber more straight, definite shapes—yes, buildings: black buildings. Were they empty? He stumbled onto a roughly beaten trail in the snow. The mare's trail; it had to be. Then, lower still, he saw, against the stars above the trees, the outline of a chimney and the fuzzy rise of furnace smoke!

He kicked his deadened feet along the broken trail. It led gradually downward. It led toward a corner shadowed by two big pole gates. Beyond one gate he saw an open yard and then the dark building with the rising smoke. Behind the other gate were the square shoulders of a huge haystack. From somewhere behind it he heard a thick drumming begin, as from horses pounding nervously about in a corral.

Morena saw him coming. She stood in the corner made by the gates, striped by the shadows of the poles and so almost invisible. She was cold and hungry and tired. Her foot still pained her every time she gave in and rested it down. She didn't want to travel anymore. She wouldn't trust herself to the man approaching. She put her head low into the corner to avoid ropes and shifted her hind end toward him.

Alex, his mind on the dim, gray smoke, saw a huge dim movement suddenly in front of him. He startled, tripped on his weak legs, and fell on his knees in the snow.

She startled because of his quick flounderings, and stumbled about almost as awkwardly as he.

"Hey! It's me, horse," Alex shouted. He made small clear sounds. "It's me. I came, too. We made it! We're safe!" With throat and tongue he shoved the words out. He realized bigger and bigger what he was saying: he was safe! All the fright was dead. "You can't get rid of me, horse. I'm a caveman. I've lived here a million years!" He was back on his feet. His joy, a feeling of tremendous strength, filled up his whole world. He forgot his numbness, the aches. He felt only his strength. He moved and crowded her so she shifted against the gate to her right. Then he trudged straight up behind her. She stood there, close to the hay beyond the gate, and not eager to try whirling back; she'd have to swing outward, weight on the paining hoof.

He crouched down and pulled the leg she kept up over to him, bringing the hoof against his knees. He had to use two hands on the knife, because each hand was too puffed and stiff to grip it alone. If she kicked he'd jump aside. He'd done it before. He dug and sliced, but didn't tap, and cut the thick splinter loose, dropped the hoof and stumbled away.

She startled again at his abruptness. The hind leg touched ground. The pain was dulled. She tried it again: it only tingled. Now she wheeled and pranced away, throwing puffs and loud squeaks from the snow, and more rattlings of her insides. She didn't go far, just far enough to feel free. She stopped and nosed back a little toward the hay.

"Go ahead! Take off. I don't care," he sent his voice at her. "Now we're even. I don't owe you a thing, horse. Go on! You led me here, but I opened the gates. I pried you loose. I did as much as you."

Then Alex stood trying to decide whether he should open the gate to the hay corral or not, and it was wonderful to have such a mild, powerful, unfrightening decision before him. He couldn't be hurt no matter how he decided. Not with the dark chimney smoke rising just beyond the yard gate. The building's blackness didn't bother him. He'd use his knife; he'd get in some way. But right now he could stand with the cold stinging him, and the dim, wild distance all around him, and feel unafraid and unbothered in it. He'd worked too hard for this feeling to let it pass too quickly.

For him now just stars and snow were light enough, and warmth enough. There were no longer the eyes of bats and hounds above him. He didn't have to snarl and run from them. The hill he'd just come down rose softly now in the starlight, every inch of a trillion inches filled with brightly-colored pinpricks of dim snow-sparkle. It was harmless, and beautiful. The rest of the hills lifted and spread out gently through his memory. He grinned back over them; they were good, because he owned them now, as much as anyone, because he knew them now like no one else could, because he'd worked his own way through them. He hadn't borrowed help from any-

body. Alex shuffled backward and sat himself down on the pile of snow that had been pushed out of the way so the big gates could open, when anyone wanted to open them. It didn't matter that his hands and feet and ears were stiff. He wanted to feel for just another moment how he could shrug off this cold, without an ounce of fear. He wanted to pleasure once again in just the nearness of warmth, in the actual discovering and conquering joy, before the warmth in that building made the realness of it fade out behind him. Alex sat uncrouched, calmly resting back and smiling for yet a moment more at the vast night he was strong enough to stand against, and so weary he never felt it come; he went to sleep on that soft backrest of snow, and the iced air immediately clamped tighter and tighter around his still body.

Morena pawed about restlessly. Her foot felt better, and the hay scent was thick, but the fence blocked her way, and she knew no where else to go. She paced back and forth, caught only by the hay scent. She stopped, and impatiently beat a foreleg at the cushioned ground. She looked up at the first flashing of light, the first low, familiar muttering. She nickered impatiently.

21

Once again Marv Hannum's thoughts had been hurrying across the hill pastures as he tried to keep his pickup on the roadway ahead. This time there was no sun glare, but rut shadows and snow sparkles danced confusingly in his headlights. Occasionally the headlights from Gene Wall's pickup flashed in his mirror.

Debbie sat beside him, her face still creased in that expression that had been on it ever since the knock on the Wall's front door: Milt Toppen, from Belle Ore, standing there, hunched up in the cold, saying a boy was missing from the Scout campout, and they'd just now discovered it.

"Marv!" Debbie had half screamed as they'd hurried out the door, past the thermometer nailed on the porch, "It's three degrees below zero!" And she'd let that speak for itself till they'd bounced across the cattle guard and onto the county roadway. Then she'd cried, "Marv, how could they? All his camping pack in that bus, and now it's below zero! Why didn't they phone? We could've started sooner!"

Too much of a hurry, or the lines out, he'd guessed, but he'd only nodded.

He was thinking of the fallen gate; he'd thought the old mare had loosened it. But why would a *boy* loosen it, instead of just crawling under? As a signal? Was it a signal that he'd turned away from? But he hadn't known anyone was missing.

Why didn't the kid walk down the roadway?

Lost in the night?

He saw fresh tire ruts turning off to the left ahead of him, where the roadway branched south to curve up into the hills, past the campground. He followed his vague old tracks in the roadway bending north.

If he'd just gone and checked that gate when he'd been up there! He'd have seen footprints—maybe.

He'd told Debbie he'd checked and found no tracks there, that he'd kept honking his horn and nothing came for feed. He'd said it was clear the old mare'd broken through ahead of the storm; she'd get hungry pawing at snow all day in the middle pasture and show up waiting at the steer lot gate the first thing in the morning, just as always. *Those searchers from town'll find that open gate at daybreak,* he thought. Who knew what tracks or marks might still be there.

They wouldn't find any of his. *I ought to get up there first.* No, finding the boy was more important.

"We'll build a signal fire, on that knoll above the corrals," he said aloud. "You and Wilma'll have to keep it going. Gene and me, we'll get a couple horses and work upward, a-yelling. He might have found shelter somewhere."

"The poor soul," she cried, dismally. "It's been all night and all day and now night again. Below zero. What hope is there?"

"It was warm during the day," he said.

"But all that country," she said. "And it's frigid now. So *you* be careful, will you."

"There's plenty of firewood, and we'll ride together," he said.

Suddenly she stirred: "Marv! You don't suppose he's found Morena! Is that why the gate was open? That wind could've covered lots of tracks. There'd be warmth to an animal like that. Maybe that's why you didn't see her coming for hay when you honked. Maybe they're somewhere together!" Her voice had brightened to almost the quality of a schoolgirl cheering in the last quarter of a football game.

"No," he bit the answer out. "He couldn't catch her. She wouldn't stand to let him mount; she'd nose her head against a tree and run over him when she'd whirl away. He'd be better off finding a cougar out there."

But he didn't know where that horse might show

127

up. What he'd told her had seemed the truth then. It most likely still was.

"Don't set yourself up dreaming," he said.

He shifted gears and aimed the pickup off the county way and up over the hump of his own cattle guard, and began steering along the lane to his yard. Around the brightness of the headlights the night seemed coal-dark; when the lights dipped downward on a gentle slope they found the house and buildings. The windows glittered like flakes of quartz and mica in huge gray rocks. He saw a shadow of his own pickup loom against them, from the lights of Gene's pickup behind.

Then they were stopped. "Better first go get yourself dressed warmer," he said to Debbie, "while we get things started out here."

Then he opened the door, and a horse's impatient nicker caught him when he had just one foot on the ground. He knew that nicker too well.

"What the—" he began. "Marv!—" Debbie gasped. And they jumped away from the pickup, went running across the snowpacked yard, without a thought of the Walls behind them, without even thinking to take the battery lantern from the cab. They skidded and dashed around the corner of the toolshed, their eyes adjusting as best they could to the misty glow of snow and stars. Raised above the gate, outlined in black against the stars, they saw the familiar angles of a long and heavy face.

"Morena!" Debbie squeaked it out.

"How did—" he began again, his voice no more than a low demanding cough.

At the gate they tried to reach her.

"Marv! There's something round her neck!"

He flung the bolt and shoved the gate open; they didn't hear the running steps of the Walls behind them, but Morena in a pestered hurry swung away from the charge of people, then in a sudden, urgent effort she awkwardly tried to dodge away from a bank of piled snow, but slipped heavily and fell.

Marv Hannum leaped to grab at the strange loop about her neck. He almost had it when he turned rigid, and stared at the snow bank. Like a horrible metal machine he slowly bent, reaching out a monster's stiff and groping hand—

"Cheer, Debbie!" he roared, when he felt the warmth that was still in the boy's face.

Morena scrambled and heaved onto her feet among them, unnoticed. She jogged off immediately, her insides rattling, her hooves thumping in the squeaking snow beneath her. Nothing chased her. She didn't go far. She stopped and turned around, her head canted off to one side to see frontwards and backwards more clearly. She watched the movements of the people with uncertainty and suspicion, with impatience and endurance.

22

AT FIRST ALEX THOUGHT HE HAD WET HIS BED. HIS hands and feet felt damp and cold.

Then they began to pain him, and his ears pained. There were a thousand spiders biting him, hornets stinging him. His eyes popped open, then clamped shut against glaring white light. He had a sensation that he was off balance, not standing up or lying down.

The biting made him toss and squirm. His face turned against a cushion suddenly behind him—only he felt jabbed by needles.

"Ow," he reacted. "Oh," he groaned out loud as he turned again, for the sharp biting made it impossible to hold still.

He stopped.

Someone had spoken to him. A man's voice.

He opened his eyes again. The light didn't seem quite as shocking. He was in a room, with blue and white wallpaper—and faces. Four faces staring at him out of the wallpaper. The faces were pasted flat to the wall. Then he saw they were not part of the wall. They were two men and two women. There were clothing colors beneath the faces.

"Easy, boy. You're all right now," the voice came again, from the man nearest him. A very thick man, with very dark hair.

"Who are you?" Alex murmured.

"Marv's my name. We're all friends."

"There wasn't anybody, anywhere," Alex murmured, not really knowing why—suddenly he was frightened that he'd spoken; he didn't know what was happening.

"The hills are full of them now." The man's voice spoke softly. "The sheriff's just gone out trying to call them back down before someone's really lost. We just talked to the highway patrol on his radio, and your folks are already on their way out here."

The man's steady voice, the words 'hills', 'highway', 'your folks', brought Alex nearer to his senses. Suddenly he remembered the dark building with the furnace smoke rising.

"Is this the ranch house?"

"You bet," said the man.

One of the women smiled suddenly. "Time to go heat up that oatmeal," she said, and began to leave.

"There weren't any lights," Alex remembered, trying hard to get his mind clear. And then the biting pains tore at him again, and he tried to roll away from them and groaned loudly in spite of himself—and found he was in a big deep chair, and that his feet were hanging down in a tub of water, and his hands and head were wrapped in towels. Now the four people closed about him again. Their mouths and eyes were thin and wrinkled.

"What's the matter with me?" he cried out.

"There's nothing. Nothing warmth won't fix," said the woman who'd talked of oatmeal. She'd started to leave, but she hadn't left. She began smiling at him.

Then the other woman was smiling at him. "We're trying to keep you cool, hon. So you won't warm up too fast."

"It hurts," he answered.

"Where?" said the dark-haired man.

"Everywhere."

"Like pins?" said the man.

"Yes."

"That's the frost coming out," the man said. "You're good and frostbit. But your feelings are coming back. You'll just have to tough this thaw out, and you'll be okay. You'll have to tough it yourself; we can't help you much."

"It hurts worse to get thawed than it does to get frozen," the other man spoke down to him. He was taller, with only a frazzling of hair on a head that was almost bald. Now he smiled a little. "You'll feel a frost coming a month away from now on, fella. But at least you'll be *able* to feel it. And run from it."

"And not get caught in a snowbank," said the woman who'd called him 'hon'. "What luck that that horse sang out to us or he'd have frozen right outside here, with all of us out looking for him."

"Morena," said the first woman. She had dark hair, too, falling straight back into a curve at the base of her neck. "Morena," she said again. "If it hadn't been for that big pole gate, I'll bet she'd have brought him right into the house and tucked him into bed. Oh, I told you we'd all end up with Morena."

"Who's Morena?" Alex asked. He was nervous about everything they were saying, and partly just trying to get his mind off his paining.

"The old mare you rode in here," the dark-haired man said. "You must be one whale of a wrangler, is all I can say. You've got to come out here sometime and teach me how to handle horses." Now the man was grinning, but his voice seemed straight. And suddenly Alex remembered the horse, the old mare—standing off with her head cocked to one side, keeping away from him, then dashing past him while he tried desperately to get her help, and kicking at him, and running off and running off and running, leaving him alone and weak in all the snow and cold and darkness. He remembered everything now.

"I—I—" he stammered, trying to get his whole

story, his old anger, his great triumph, all out at once.

The dark-haired grinning man didn't wait. "You know what," he laughed. "I'm going to tell you something I wouldn't tell anyone but my wife and Gene and Wilma, here. That horse wouldn't come in with the roundup, so I had to go up there special, with the best horse I've got, and after two days I still couldn't get near her. You've got to be part monkey just to get near her in a corral. She'd be too slow and stumbly now, if I tried to *use* her for anything. She's just all problem. All I wanted was to catch her just once more so I could ship her to market. So I shut the gates and left her up there to starve her down enough so I could get hold of her. I went up there today, on top of all this snow, to get her with fresh hay. But I couldn't find hide nor hair again. I came back telling Debbie that death itself couldn't catch her, or figure out how to get on her if it did. And here all the while she lets you catch her afoot, with nothing but a belt, and you ride right to the back door." Then he just broke out into a big smiling chuckle, and the other man and the women joined in.

"Marv, you just never *had* to catch her *bad* enough," said the taller man; and the woman who'd called him 'hon' said, "Well, just look how wonderful it's worked out. The luckiest thing you've ever done was to close those gates, Marv. Imagine a boy like this trying to walk out all that way. He couldn't have done it!"

"Morena always did work when she was needed!" the other woman exclaimed happily.

Then Alex began to laugh, too, because they were getting it so wrong, and because it was easier to try forgetting the thawing pains that way than by complaining; and because he, too, had been left to freeze and starve, and it was no fun to remember the hunger and anger and fright, and so much better to be safe and warm and laughing.

So he told only of how the snow had sealed his shelter that first night, and how he'd seen the miracle of a horse in the daylight. He told of the tall, powerful feeling on her shoulders after he'd teased her with handfuls of grass, and climbed on with a ladder of cut hair. He told of the bits of warmth beneath her her mane; he said how the stars and highway lights had kept him from feeling lost but that it was the horse that had to show him where the gates were, only he'd had to keep her moving slow because the snow kept balling under her hooves and making her limp. He told them how there'd been creatures walking over those hills for millions of years, and how all that time the Swan had kept her wings spread in the Milky Way. He told them of the steamy warmth of the steers, and how it'd felt so good to see the chimney smoke that he'd just sat down and relaxed—and deep in the big chair Alex remembered the joy of coming down that last hill and finding warmth so near. The memory felt so good he didn't try to talk or think any further. He sat, with their voices drifting past him, trying harder and harder to feel it all again as clearly as he had before. Without knowing it he slipped back into a tired, dreamless sleep, before any oatmeal could come.

23

THE HORSE QUIETLY EATING FROM THE WAGON
that was piled high with hay for the morning's early
feeding, was all alone, because the fluster of people
had gone off and left the gate from the steer lot open.

She saw two men come out from amid the lights
in one of the buildings. She saw them cross the yard,
squeaking the snow with each step, and disappear
behind another building. She heard the creaking and
clunk of a gate closing. She saw the men come back.
She heard their sudden voices and saw the quick
movements pointing toward her. She saw them disappear into the dark insides of another building.
Alertly, she kept on eating.

The men came back again and kept moving toward her. Now they moved slowly. One held out
something that shone dimly and looked familiar, and

soon was close enough for its scent to reach her. The pail of oats smelled good—but the hay was free and Morena didn't want to be handled or worked. She moved away.

The men moved apart; they showed ropes, and she knew what ropes were. Now whenever they moved she whirled and ducked her head. They crowded her toward the flat, solid wall of a building. She raised her head, sniffed sharply and started to run between them. At the first movement of their arms she stopped short. The loops flicked out and fell emptily across each other in the snow in front of her. She swung to one side and loped around behind one of the men and to the other side of the hay wagon. She paused to snatch a mouthful.

Gene Wall yipped with laughter. "What a clown! We'll have to get the boy to help us."

"I'd rather get a gun," Marv Hannum grumbled.

Morena dodged them again, and again.

"There's a gun right in that pickup!" Marv Hannum growled.

"You can't do that," Gene Wall said. "Not after she's brought that boy in."

"I know I can't," said Marv Hannum. "Now I'm going to have to feed her and chase her around till she decides she's old enough to quit living. I'll bet that's another twenty years."

"Doesn't look like she's going to be any trouble, as long as you keep a load of feed out for her. Maybe

you can lead her into the corral with the wagon in the morning."

"Meanwhile she won't scatter more than half of what she eats here, either. But I suppose if we keep running her in the dark she'll bump into something and I'll have a doctoring problem. Be easier to throw on some more hay."

"I think maybe we'd better leave her alone. Or we'll have to thaw each other out. She isn't going to go anywhere tonight, not with all that hay sitting there."

"I know it," said Marv Hannum. He coiled up his rope and put it, for tomorrow's convenience, in the cab of the pickup. "But it's just bad management."

Morena kept concentrating on the men. Even when they disappeared back inside the lighted building, she stayed still at the edge of the yard, looking forward and back, until, feeling assured, she ambled forward and began eating again, till she was full.

Then she went and stood with her back end against a flat, solid building, sheltered from the plains breeze that would occasionally scratch through the sparkling air, stirring the brittle, flaky snow, blurring all footprints and crusting them shut. Morena lowered her head in the deeper lee of her shoulders, and, drawing warmth from the hay she'd eaten, she stood free, and asleep.